Rink

MW01181207

Northern Nightmare

Tom Mohrbach

Published by Tom Mohrbach, 2020.

Also by Tom Mohrbach

Vatican Vengeance
Cardinal Deceit

Standalone
Vatican Vengeance
Northern Nightmare

Watch for more at https://tommohrbach.com.

This book is dedicated to everyone that enjoys nature in its rawest form.

CHAPTER 1

Karl regarded the dead body in his driveway the way most folks looked at road-kill. It was something to be dealt with before it stunk too bad, or the turkey vultures decided to congregate for a feast, but for now, it could wait. It was lunchtime. He maneuvered his Gator, a 4-wheel ATV, around the corpse and continued down the dirt two-track that led to his ramshackle house.

Jesse, flipping through an old Penthouse magazine, sat in an old green velour La-Z-Boy on the small porch with his boots resting on the wood rail. The stairs and porch that fronted the house were well past their prime but the ramshackle house was even older.

Karl killed the Gator's engine and asked, "Who's that up the driveway?"

"Hell if I know," Jesse replied without taking his gaze from the magazine. Jesse, barely 20, was Karl's half-brother. They shared the same father.

"Unless I'm wrong, it sure looked like one of your arrows sticking out of his back."

"I didn't say I didn't shoot the guy; just said I don't know who he is."

Karl climbed the three rickety stairs to the porch, being careful to avoid the middle step as it was almost rotted through, and smacked Jesse's feet from the rail.

Buttlicker, Jesse's huge mongrel that sprawled out on the porch next to him, emitted a low, menacing growl while his ears flattened against his head.

"That mutt ever comes after me, I'll kill it," Karl promised. "Now don't play stupider than you is, dickhead! What happened?"

Jesse regarded Karl with brooding eyes while patting Buttlicker's head before replying, "I guess he cain't read our signs. The sumbitch was banging on the door before I was even dressed. Wouldn't stop either. I went out the back door and when I came around the front he was still pounding on the damn door, so I shot him. Must have hit his spine 'cause he fell backward off the porch and couldn't stand. He started crawling down the driveway. He was crying and moaning like a wounded deer. I cut his throat so he wouldn't suffer no more."

Karl picked up a clipboard from the porch floor. A bunch of papers with *Census* printed across the top were attached to it. "Well, shit! He sure as hell didn't walk here. Where's his ride?"

"I stashed it in the barn. Harley should be able to get some good coin for the parts."

"You best git him off the damn driveway before Harley gets here. He'll be pissed. I'm starving. I'm gonna fix me a liverwurst and onion sandwich. You want one?"

"Hell yes. Put some of that spicy mustard on it, too."

Karl nodded and entered the home.

Sue Ellen, affectionately known as "Sexy Susie," was sitting on the faux leather sofa, wearing only a pink thong and an extra-large white T-shirt. She drank a can of Busch Light and watching Fox News. "Can you believe the damn Democrats are still whining 'bout Trump? Don't they see all the good he's done?"

"Good Lord, woman, put some clothes on. Jesse is on the porch looking at them nude gals in Penthouse. What d'you think he thinks when he sees you dressed like that after looking at all those titties?"

Sue Ellen smiled and lifted her T-shirt. "Ain't nothin in that magazine better than these. You worried your little brother is gonna have a go at me?"

Karl shook his head. "No, but he is still a man and you don't need to walk around nearly bare-ass in front of him. Now put on some damn pants."

Sue Ellen stood and pushed out her lower lip while sauntering to the bedroom. Karl admired her figure as he always did. He had to admit she had incredible tits and the rest of her wasn't bad either. She worked out four days a week on a stripper pole in the barn and punched the heavy bag too. He wasn't sure how long she would stick around but the last three years were the best of his life. He would marry her in a minute, but so far she had refused his near-weekly proposals.

A few minutes later, Karl was spreading the spicy mustard on the sandwiches when Sue Ellen walked out of the bedroom wearing hip-hugging gray sweatpants with the words "sweet cheeks" stenciled on the rear in bright pink. She had the same T-shirt on but had it knotted tight above her midriff, the thin cotton stretched taut across her ample breasts. Her bleach-blonde hair was pulled back tightly in a short ponytail secured with a rubber-band. She was barefoot, as she always was around the house and yard.

"Better?" she asked while doing a slow pirouette.

"A little. I guess."

She smiled sexily at him, then looked at the liverwurst and frowned.

"You hungry?" Karl asked.

"Not for that crap," she said while reaching around his waist and squeezing his groin.

Karl moaned and said, "Damn, girl, at least let me eat first. I'm starving."

"That mouth of yours ain't going nowhere near my lips after you eat that shit."

"Aww, man. Okay. I'll eat it later, but take this one out to Jesse, would ya?"

"Sure. I'll see you in the bedroom. Be ready," she said while picking up the paper plate with the sandwich and some corn chips on it.

Jesse was still seated in the La-Z-Boy sipping a can of Busch Light when Sue Ellen brought the lunch to him. He laid the Penthouse down and took the plate, grinning at her. She looked nervously over her shoulder to make certain Karl didn't follow her outside and whispered, "I'm going to screw your brother now, but I'll be thinking of you, baby, while I do. You were so good this morning. Don't forget, it's our secret." Sue Ellen winked at him and walked back into the house.

Jesse finished up his sandwich and corn chips, as well as his fourth beer of the day. He was pissing off the front porch as Harley, his oldest brother, pulled up in his wrecker.

"Who the fuck is that in the driveway?" Harley yelled as he jumped from the truck.

Jesse finished taking a leak and zipped up quickly. "Some asshole that cain't read our signs, He was pounding on the door this morning like he was a cop or something, so I shot 'im with my bow."

Harley shook his head and breathed in deeply. "You plan on leaving him there all fucking day?"

"No. I just ain't got around to moving him yet."

"Well, get around to doing it before someone comes looking for him. What did he want?"

"I guess he was taking a survey or something."

"Shit, Jesse. You can't just go shootin' everyone that comes up to our damn door. Now that's twice in six months."

"But he was trespassing, Harley. Damn, how many signs we got to put up before they believe us? This is America, after all. Sue Ellen says we got rights to defend our property. She's smart about that stuff."

Harley climbed the three stairs, avoiding the middle one, and sat down in the wooden rocking chair opposite the La-Z-Boy. He sighed and said, "Listen to me. The next time someone trespasses just tell them to leave. If they don't, then shoot them, but at least give them a chance to leave, okay?"

"Well, okay. If that's what you want."

"It is, brother. Now tell me, what kind of vehicle did we get?"

Jesse smiled and said, "A real nice 2012 Ford F-150."

Harley stood and walked over to Jesse, patting him on the shoulder. "Well, at least that's good news. Come on, I'll help you carry him over to the barn. You and I can butcher him up there and feed him to the pigs, then we'll get started on taking the pickup apart. Is Karl around?"

"Yeah, he's inside riding Sue Ellen."

"Damn, that girl sure is energetic." Harley wondered for the hundredth time what she was doing with a loser like his brother Karl.

CHAPTER 2

Officer Mitchell "Mitch" Manning handcuffed a screaming husband inside a filthy kitchen on the east side of his patrol district while stepping around a pile of spaghetti noodles on the floor. A red splatter of sauce dripped from the wall, several strands of noodles still clinging lightly to it six feet above the pile, not unlike a headshot wound exit spray.

Mitch was glad no shots were fired at this domestic disturbance, but the husband's wife was none too happy about him throwing a plate of spaghetti at her—especially one that she had so lovingly prepared just minutes earlier. "That's right! Take the son-of-a-bitch to jail," she screamed, while Mitch's backup, officer Andrea Kosloski, attempted to keep her in the living room.

"Screw you, bitch. I'll be out tomorrow," the husband hissed back.

"Alright, that's enough from both of you!" Officer Manning ordered. At 6'2" and almost 215 pounds, with broad shoulders and large arms, he usually was listened to. It was many years since he helped lead his highschool football team to a divisional championship with a record-setting season of sacks, forced fumbles, and recoveries, but he was still in great shape despite being only two years shy of 50.

When the husband started to protest, Mitch began to escort him towards the front door, while his cell phone began to vibrate in his shirt pocket. He ignored the persistent vibration and continued directing the handcuffed suspect towards the front door.

7

"Throw a plate of spaghetti at me again, asshole! Maybe I'll go next door to Donnie's tonight while you're locked up and see what a real man feels like. He's been looking at my ass since we moved in," the wife hollered from the dining room.

"Andrea, if she says another word, cuff her up for interfering," Mitch said.

The husband suddenly dropped low and pivoted to his left, causing Mitch to lose his grip on him. He hopped upwards and swept his handcuffs under his feet with the agility of a gymnast and charged towards his wife in the living room. Officer Andrea's back was facing towards him as she shooed the wife back into the dining room.

Mitch shouted a warning to Andrea, but it was too late. The husband shouldered her out of the way with the force of a fullback, knocking her sideways and into a cheap china cabinet. The glass doors and china shattered while Andrea fell to the floor. The husband now had his hands around his wife's neck and was choking her as she spat on him.

Mitch cursed and yanked his Taser from his utility belt. He flipped the switch to on while aiming the red laser light in the middle of the suspect's back. He realized the wife was also going to get the jolt but figured she deserved that for continuing to escalate the situation. He smoothly pulled back the trigger.

The two darts instantly found their mark. Both husband and wife went rigid for a few seconds while riding the current then screamed and fell to the floor. Once the five-second ride was over, Officer Andrea hauled the husband off the floor with a handful of his hair. Mitch, who knew some payback was coming, quickly turned to his right so that his bodycam wouldn't capture the incident. He noticed that Andrea's bodycam was on the floor, apparently falling off her shirt when she was shoved into the cabinet.

Andrea smoothly spun the husband around to face her and head-butted him in his nose. The crunch of bone and cartilage resulted in a steady flow of blood from the suspect's nose. "Oh, damn. It looks like you busted your nose when you fell to the floor," she said with mock concern. "Be careful you don't trip down the porch steps, too."

Mitch smiled to himself as Andrea escorted the husband roughly past him.

"You okay?"

"I'm fine, but the china cabinet wasn't so lucky," Andrea quipped back.

"I'm guessing you want this arrest?"

"Absolutely!" She answered with a devilish smile. "Besides, you're leaving for your hunting trip tomorrow morning. I doubt you want to be here typing all night."

"Trust me, I'm not complaining. I owe you one."

"You bet your ass you do, and I intend to collect," Andrea said with a coy look.

Several minutes later, after calming down the suspect's wife, Mitch was back in his patrol car catching up on his daily patrol-log when his cell phone started to vibrate again. He snatched it from his pocket and saw three missed calls from his oldest brother, Luke, as well as two texts. Both texts simply read, *Call me.*

Mitch hit recall and Luke answered on the second ring.

"Hey, brother, you busy?" inquired Luke.

"Sorry. I wasn't ignoring you. I told you I worked until seven, and, yeah, it's been a busy shift."

"Sorry bro, but just think, starting tomorrow you'll be off for seven straight days."

"Actually, starting in about 15 minutes, I'll be off seven straight days. What's up?"

Luke sighed. *Not a good sign,* Mitch thought. "Troy called. He missed his flight from Vegas. He couldn't reschedule until tomorrow morning, so he wants us to pick him up at the Detroit airport at 9 a.m. tomorrow."

Mitch was pissed. This was typical Troy. "Not a chance, brother. We planned on leaving at 7 a.m. sharp like we always do. He can rent his own damn car and meet us up there."

"Look. We're only leaving a couple of hours later, it's not that far out of the way. He'll be at the curb; we won't even have to go in," reasoned Luke.

"But he won't be at the curb," Mitch said. "He'll have some excuse like he always does. Besides, it's still four more hours north. We won't even get to the cabin until one at the earliest. Probably later because he'll insist on stopping somewhere for breakfast."

Luke sighed again. "Mitch, it's the only week we all get together anymore. Dad's been gone for almost five years now. We can make this work. If not for us, for Dad. We don't need to hunt tomorrow night anyhow. This way we can unpack, relax with a few beers, and enjoy a campfire. We got all week to hunt. It'll be okay."

"Alright, but he had better be at the damn curb. You tell him that. If he isn't, he's on his own for transportation."

"Thanks, brother. I'll tell him. Bless you, bro. See ya in the morning, probably at 8 a.m. instead of seven. At least we'll have a bit more rest."

Mitch grunted an acknowledgment and disconnected. He hammered out a text to their younger brother, Ryan. *We'll be a bit later tomorrow. Troy missed his flight. Big surprise!!! New ETA at your place will be 11:30-noon. See you then bro.*

The response was almost immediate. *No problem. Preacher already told me. I guess since we haven't heard different, Troy didn't fare too well in the tournament.*

Preacher was the nick-name they gave their oldest brother, Luke. The four brothers, as well as their two sisters, were all raised strict Catholics. Luke, now 60, was ordained a Deacon after he retired from a 25-year stint in the Army.

Mitch shook his head before sending the next text. Troy was in Vegas for yet another poker tournament. He fancied himself a professional gambler but more often than not was on the losing end. "No doubt. See you tomorrow," he texted back.

Huh. Mitch thought. *If his other two brothers weren't upset about it why the hell was he?* He glanced at his watch and swore. He was off shift in 5 minutes and wasn't even at the station yet. He gunned the patrol car away from the curb and sped toward the station.

• • • •

CHAPTER 3

Harley wasn't always bad. His birth name was Harlan T. Rowson. He was a fairly happy little toddler. He was the second child of Edward and Sandra Rowson. Edward's great-great-grandfather had emigrated from a small community outside of Herefordshire, England to settle in Michigan, where he found steady work in the booming logging industry. Michigan at the time was offering land for as little as $1.25 an acre, providing the purchaser agreed to work in the logging industry and sign a one-year contract.

Harley's great-grandfather chose the tract of land that Harley and his brothers currently inhabited, but Harley's father, Edward Rowson, sold over a hundred acres of it back to the state several years earlier when money was hard to come by.

Edward Rowson had struggled to find steady work and eventually purchased a service station in Mio. Sandra was Edward's first cousin and she had suffered from undiagnosed schizophrenia. She drowned her first child, Amber, in their bathtub on her first birthday, but told her husband it was an accident. The authorities didn't have a reason to suspect otherwise.

A year later, Harley was born, and Sandra heard voices telling her to let this one live. Harley was followed six years later by Karl. Because of her untreated mental illness, Sandra was a terrible mother. She self-medicated with heavy alcohol use. The two boys basically raised themselves when their father was working, which was 12 hours a day, six days a week.

Sandra got progressively worse and harbored illusions that her children were evil entities intending to harm her. To prevent them from such activity she would lock them in their dingy basement for most of the day and release them just before their father returned home. When Karl was a newborn, she would toss down a bottle for Harley to give to him, and a granola bar for Harley, unless she forgot. Her memory wasn't very good.

Harley got used to the dark days of confinement, with only a single bulb providing any illumination. He would hold his little brother to keep him from crying and assure him everything would be okay. A rat soon became his pet. He would even share a small portion of his granola bar with it. Spiders also became his friends, and he would trap them in a mason jar to play with them later. He would relieve himself in a bucket that his mother made him empty every day back in the woods.

Harley was happy when the school year started. It was such a relief not to be holed up in the basement with only Karl, the rats, and spiders for friends. Unfortunately, his social skills were severely lacking, and his behavior was far from stellar. When he turned seven and attended second grade, he would yell, bite, and hit other students, as well as teachers.

The teachers began to suspect neglect or abuse, but this was the mid-1960's before most public schools had counselors. Their suspicions were never reported to any authorities other than the principal. Sandra and Ed dutifully attended parent-teacher meetings and acted dismayed at their son's behavior. Mr. Rowson was very strict with the punishment he doled out for little Harley afterward. Belt whippings, and worse, were commonplace for Harley.

Harley repeatedly complained to his father about how he and his brother were being treated while he was working, but he refused to believe them and punished him even more severely for telling lies about his mother. His mother not only locked him in his room after school but now warned him if he ever complained to his father again she would kill him and his brother.

Harley believed her. His resentment for her turned to hatred, and over the course of six additional years, became a simmering rage. On Harley's 13th birthday, a Saturday, he refused to enter the basement after breakfast.

His mother again ordered him to do so but he didn't budge. A growing boy, he now stood defiantly eye-to-eye with his mother. Karl had dutifully gone down the basement stairs already. Harley was whip-thin from malnutrition while she was fifty pounds overweight. He had not defied her in over a year, and when he had done so in the past, she would simply drag him down the stairs and then lock him in the basement.

As his mother approached to grab him, he quickly side-stepped to her left, then forcibly shoved her down the basement stairs. She gasped and flailed for the handrail that Harley had spent the previous day loosening with a butterknife. It easily gave way and she somersaulted headfirst down the steep wooden stairs. At the bottom, she slammed her forehead onto the dirty cement floor.

After a few seconds, she groggily managed to get to her hands and knees. She hadn't even heard Harley follow her down. As she saw his legs in front of her, she looked up and observed that he was holding a long board. As she wiped the blood away from a cut on her forehead, she thought that

Harley looked truly happy for the first time in a long time. He was grinning from ear to ear.

It was her last thought as Harley wound the board back, like a baseball player with a bat at the plate, and swung it fast and low into her forehead. The resulting sound was not unlike a solid hit that would surely be a home run.

Karl saw the whole thing. Harley put a finger to his lips and told him never to tell anyone. He assured his little brother that he would never allow anyone to lock them in the basement again.

The medical examiner later ruled the death accidental, as a result of falling down the basement steps, and the police closed the investigation. Harley's father was skeptical. Harley seemed indifferent to his mother's death and in fact seemed happier in the days following.

Harley's father took a new bride a year later. His new bride was much younger and was actually his niece. She tried to assert some authority over Harley and his brother, but always backed down when Harley refused to obey her. She complained to her husband that the boy had some seriously bad vibes. Six years later, she became pregnant and Jesse was born.

Jesse carried some of the same DNA as Harley's first wife and his two half-brothers. From the onset, he enjoyed harming animals, except for dogs. He loved dogs. Jesse didn't hunt or trap for food, or to sell fur, like the vast majority of hunters. He did those activities because he enjoyed hurting things, He truly loved to see animals suffer. As he aged, he discovered that he enjoyed hurting people even more than he did animals. He was a bad seed that grew worse each year.

The Rowson brothers were meant for each other, as well as for the backwoods where their encounters with tourists were limited. Unfortunately for the Manning brothers, their paths would soon cross.

CHAPTER 4

Troy was halfway into his non-stop flight from Vegas to Detroit. He paid a few bucks extra for an aisle seat, but the cramped economy airline seats were still far from comfortable. Thankfully, two unhappy babies had finally stopped crying. He needed a smoke bad, not the vape thing, but the real cancer-stick with maximum nicotine. At 6 a.m., the cabin was darkened and most of the passengers were sleeping or at least resting. Troy undid his seatbelt and stood in the aisle, stretching his thin, wiry frame.

"Excuse me, sir," a sultry voice said quietly behind him.

He turned towards the voice and looked into the gorgeous green eyes of the stewardess that brought him both his Bloody Marys earlier. She squeezed by him and in doing so brushed her hip across his. She smelled like lavender. It may have been wishful thinking, but he thought she purposely initiated the contact. She murmured a "sorry" as it happened and continued up the aisle.

Hell, being 50 wasn't so bad, he thought. He still had all his hair and most of it was still brown, but the grays were coming quicker. His age and perpetual 5 o'clock shadow on his square jaw, combined with his tad-too-long hair, seemed to be the right combination for a certain type of woman.

That type was the semi-attractive, middle-aged, recent divorcee, looking to simply have fun. His stewardess seemed to fit the requirements although he wasn't certain about her marital status. He did notice she wasn't wearing a wedding ring.

Twice divorced, Troy was not the least interested in a steady relationship. After his second divorce three years ago, he was shocked to learn that most of the middle-aged women were of the same mindset. And, even better, casual sex was more accepted now than before his first marriage.

Troy walked to the rear bathroom to make room for more alcohol. Upon exiting, the same stewardess, Kristina, as her nameplate stated, was pouring a cup of coffee into a paper cup inside the galley about a foot to his right. She smiled at him.

Troy went on the offensive. *What the hell,* he thought. Hip contact and now a big smile; what did he need, a flashing neon sign? "Good morning."

"Good morning," she replied in that same sultry voice. Her long dark eyelashes and perfectly stenciled eyebrows highlighted her emerald eyes.

"You have the prettiest eyes I've ever seen," Troy said. "I know that sounds like a cheesy pickup line but I'm serious."

Kristina blushed a shade and broke eye contact before saying, "Thank you. It's not cheesy at all." After a short pause, she inquired, "Would you like some coffee?"

"Coffee sounds great. Would you think less of me if I asked for a shot of Kahlua in it?"

She laughed and said, "Not at all. I wish I could oblige but the best I can offer is bourbon. I could use some myself but that'll have to wait."

Bingo, Troy thought, then plunged ahead. "Maybe sometime, when you're not working," he suggested.

Kristina now made eye contact again and said, "That sounds great. I'll leave you my email when I deliver your coffee. Are you headed home?"

Troy had to think about that for a second. Michigan indeed was his birth home and was his actual home for 30 years, but the last 20 were split between Vegas and Atlantic City. His current residence was a crappy condo in Atlantic City, but could be lost if he didn't place highly in a big tournament soon. The bill collectors were circling like vultures.

"Yeah, I'm headed home. I come back home every October to go hunting with my brothers."

Kristina frowned. "You kill animals?"

Uh-oh, Troy thought. He needed to implement damage control, and quickly. "Not at all. Truth be told, I'm the world's worst hunter. I haven't shot a deer in twenty years. I go mainly for the time with my family and I really enjoy the outdoors."

"Guns make me nervous."

"Me too. That's why I'm strictly a bowhunter." Troy lied. He loved guns, especially pistols. He owned five of them. His favorite was a 1902 American Eagle Luger-Fat Barrel that he worried he may have to pawn soon. Kristina perked up.

"You bow hunt? I loved archery. My Dad taught me how to shoot. I was competitive for a bit."

"Really? How cool is that," Troy said and hoped he salvaged the situation.

A few minutes later, when Kristina delivered his coffee and a mini-bottle of bourbon, he noticed her email on the napkin and realized he still had the touch. He thought about Kristina for a few minutes as he sipped his coffee, mostly carnal thoughts, before his mind wandered to the upcoming hunt.

There is something almost mystical about northern Michigan. Michigan residents, or Michiganders, know this well. The majority of the population occupies the lower half of the lower peninsula. The large urban areas such as Detroit, Flint, and Grand Rapids are non-existent "Up North." Most of the vast area is state and national forest lands, interspersed with popular touristy towns the likes of Traverse City, Alpena, Ludington, Mackinac Island, and many others that draw thousands of out-of-staters each summer.

The first two weeks of November mark almost every Michigander's calendar as thousands of hunters invade the northern reaches of the state in pursuit of the plentiful white-tail deer. This two-week period is vital for many small northern communities that rely on tourism dollars that have slowed from the summer rush.

Troy was happy that his father had been a bow and arrow hunter. He passed his love of this pursuit onto his boys. Each October, before the woods were invaded by thousands of rifle hunters, they went bow hunting and enjoyed a much quieter, serene, almost holistic atmosphere communing with nature.

Despite being raised a Catholic, and hauled off to Sunday mass each week, the seed didn't take. He believed in God but didn't feel the need to go to church or ponder the next life.

Troy's mother, Rose, and two older sisters, Rebecca and Susan, didn't partake in the annual hunt. Instead, the women spent a long weekend enjoying Frankenmuth, a small historic German village that boasted the world's largest Christmas Store: Bronners. Frankenmuth was equally known for its world-famous chicken dinners. Hundreds of dinners were served daily in two rivaling banquet-style Bavarian-themed restaurants. Each year, the Manning brothers stopped for one of those chicken dinners on their way home to Adrian. Troy's mouth watered at the thought of the super-moist, crispy out-side, tender inside, perfectly seasoned fried chicken.

Somewhere along the way, Troy slipped into a deep sleep and dreamt of the upcoming hunt. He was tracking a nice buck when the ample blood trail he was following, through a thick stand of pines and birch trees, led to a quickly flowing river. The water appeared red. Troy dipped his hands in the cool wa-ter and recoiled when he realized it was a river of blood. He spotted a camouflage-clad body floating by face-down and rec-ognized with horror that it was his brother Mitch. His broth-er Preacher suddenly appeared on the far riverbank and was shouting something but Troy couldn't hear what he was saying. A flock of at least 100 ugly crows landed in the pine trees above him. They were incredibly loud with the constant cry of "caw, caw, caw."

Ryan now also floated by, flailing in the middle of the river, fighting the strong current. The crows suddenly went quiet as though a switch was thrown. Troy could hear Ryan screaming, "Help me, brother, help me!" as he reached out to Troy. Preach-er on the far side was screaming, "Run Troy, run, save yourself because we're already dead."

A freak of a man emerged from the woods carrying a blood-stained machete in his right hand. In his left was an arm that Troy just noticed Preacher was missing. Powerful hands from behind Troy grabbed his head and forced it into the river of blood, trying to drown him. Troy began screaming. Some-one was yelling his name.

Troy awakened to Kristina gently shaking his shoulder and saying, "Troy, Troy, wake up." Half-awake, he batted her hand away and started to push himself up from his seat when he realized he was no longer dreaming.

"Easy, take it easy, you were having a nightmare," she reassured him. The old woman seated next to him was leaning as far away from him as she could while her husband had his arm protectively around her, glaring at Troy.

"I'm sorry. I'm sorry," Troy stammered as he tried to shake off the effects of the dream, but his heart was hammering, and his body was drenched in a cold sweat. Kristina smiled reassuringly but looked concerned as she walked away while the pilot announced for everyone to prepare for landing.

Troy hadn't had a nightmare since he was in middle school. In fact, he rarely dreamed.

His fellow passengers let out a collective groan when the pilot announced it was currently 41 degrees with light rain and welcomed them to Detroit. A few minutes later, as he slowly followed the other passengers down the crowded narrow aisle towards the plane's exit, he felt like a lamb being led to slaughter.

CHAPTER 5

Ryan packed his Nissan Frontier for the trip. He was the youngest of the Manning brothers at 32 years old. His adoptive brothers and sisters were all at least 16 years older. His actual parents were tragically killed in an airplane crash while flying a short commuter flight from Detroit to Chicago. Fortunately, Ryan, an only child and a toddler at the time, was staying with his mother's sister, Mrs. Manning. The Mannings later legally adopted Ryan and raised him as their own.

Ryan didn't look anything like his siblings. His collar-length, red hair was the first clue he was adopted, as the other Manning siblings' hair was varying shades of brown, or at least had been. Preacher, currently bald, sported a close-cropped gray beard and mustache. Mitch wore what was left of his hair in a perpetual buzz cut. Troy had shaggy caramel-colored hair and wore it in a classic Beatles cut. Ryan, the runt of the Manning men at just 5'5", was a full five inches shorter than Troy and Preacher. Mitch had the height in the family at 6'2". All the Manning brothers were fairly fit with different athletic backgrounds.

Ryan placed his favorite fly rod, a Sage 8-weight with an Orvis reel, in the bed of the truck, knowing that Mitch would give him hell for it. His brothers were dedicated bow-hunters. Ryan enjoyed hunting too, but their rental cabin was close to the Ausable River and its many tributaries. He wouldn't be able to resist skipping a hunt or two for a morning of trout fishing.

He suspected some nice Browns would still be in the deeper holes, as well as some Rainbows. His rod was a bit heavy for the Rainbows but exactly right for the Browns. He was anxious to try out some of his hand-tied flies. Ryan loved to hunt as much as his brothers did, but fly fishing was his true passion.

The bed of the pickup was stuffed with gear: waders, landing net, two tree stands, a ground blind, a crossbow, compound bow, a 12-gauge pump, campfire gear, and an assortment of other necessities. Almost half of it belonged to Troy but was stored at Ryan's place as it was too costly to fly back and forth each year.

It was understood that Troy would ride up with Ryan the remainder of the trip, as Mitch and Troy couldn't tolerate each other the entire ride. Ryan was fine with that. He enjoyed Troy's company, except for his smoking. He hoped all was well thus far with Mitch and Troy. The drive to his house from the airport was only 30 minutes. Hopefully, Preacher could run interference that long.

Mitch and Troy were always like oil and water, but their relationship took a severe turn when Troy slept with Mitch's first fiancée over 25 years ago. If not for their father, who was still alive then, the relationship would never have been salvaged, even to the fragile point it was currently at. It was a semi-miracle to get them together each camp, but their father, who succumbed to a nasty prolonged bout of cancer several years earlier, had made each of the boys promise to continue their annual hunt together.

The camps were restorative and, in some ways, healing. Each of the Manning brothers looked forward to the annual trip as excitedly as they had Christmas when they were kids. Their nightly campfire discussions, solitude in the tree stands, and card games enjoyed with a few beers and bourbons were better than any amount of traditional therapy.

Ryan finished packing and fired off a text to Troy asking for an update. Troy responded almost immediately stating they were about 15 minutes away. Ryan's four-year-old Beagle, Snoop Dawg, wandered over to him and barked. He scratched him on the head and said, "Sorry, boy. Not this trip. You need to stay with Frankie and keep her company."

As if on cue, Frankie, Ryan's fiancée, exited their rustic log home and walked over to him. "I still can't believe you're leaving me for a whole week," she said with an exaggerated sadness.

"Come on, babe. I told you before, this is an annual tradition. If you're joining the Manning family you need to accept that. Besides, you get a weekend in Frankenmuth with my Mom and sisters."

Frankie rolled her eyes and said, "Great! A weekend of judgment and critiques from the Manning women."

"Relax. They love you like a sister already."

"Hmm... If you say so."

"Remember to call Jerry if you have any problems. Cell service is pretty sketchy up there, but I'll try to call or text every day."

Jerry was the nearest neighbor a quarter mile down the road. Ryan had purchased a nice tract of country land two years ago that was surrounded by farmland. It felt almost as remote as being farther north, but the city of Northville was only a twenty-minute drive. Frankie worked as a nurse at the Henry Ford Medical Center in Novi and Ryan was a District Manager for Lowes.

They both heard the sound of tires crunching on gravel as Snoop Dawg started to bark. Mitch's black suburban appeared from the pines and stopped abruptly a few yards away.

A flock of crows suddenly gathered in the pines overhead, and their raucous "caw, caw, caw" unnerved Frankie. She felt a strange sense of foreboding as Ryan walked toward his brother's SUV but soon forgot about it as her soon-to-be husband's brothers all took turns hugging her.

It was only later, after the men had left to continue their journey north, that she remembered that a flock of crows is properly referred to as a murder. Goosebumps pimpled her arms as she involuntarily shivered. Frankie resisted the urge to call Ryan and tell him to be careful as she didn't want to seem overprotective. It was a decision she would later regret.

CHAPTER 6

The barn, situated about fifty yards behind the house, was a weathered gray, two-story wood structure with an attached metal three-car garage. Harley, besides owning a semi-legitimate car repair and salvage business, passed on to him from his alcoholic father, utilized the barn for the not-so-legitimate aspects of his business. Parting out stolen cars was best conducted in privacy, not in plain sight. The barn offered plenty of that. His legit business was located on the outskirts of Mio, a small rural town located 15 miles west of his residence.

The 20 acres that the house and barn were situated on was located in the middle of the Huron-Manistee National Forest. The property was bordered by Dogman Swamp. Although technically open to hunting, not many ventured too far into it due to a thick tangle of blown over pine trees from an F-2 tornado that ripped across the area in 2011.

Despite the nearly impenetrable swamp, Harley and his brothers had erected a six feet chain link fence around the entire perimeter of their property that was topped with barbed wire. The fencing had been stolen from a public elementary school construction site near Lansing several years ago.

Attached to the fence every 20 feet were no trespassing signs. The only entrance to the property was the long two-track driveway. It was normally secured with a long metal pole on a swivel post, not unlike those used in third-world border crossings. A large plywood sign was tacked to a nearby pine warning that trespassers would be shot.

Harley and Jesse were currently in the corrugated metal section of the barn. This section was for processing meat rather than parting out cars. In just a few weeks, when firearm deer season opened, Jesse and Karl would practically be living in it as they processed deer for local hunters at very reasonable rates. They also had a reputation for having the best deer jerky and sausage around. Karl had worked for several years at a well-known meat market before being fired for stealing most of the prime cuts.

The last two weeks of November and until Christmas were the only time that they opened their property to the public. Harley had argued strenuously against it when Karl first suggested it almost six years ago. Karl, recently terminated from his meat market job, was looking for extra income to help with the bills, something Harley was always on his case about. It was ultimately a financial decision.

Karl convinced Harley that with Jesse's help, the two of them could bring in several thousand dollars processing deer in just six weeks. Karl pointed out that during that time, Harley could just focus on legitimate business. Harley reluctantly agreed, but after several years of steady income from the side business was pleased with the decision.

The butcher-style meat saw whined as Jesse, clad in white apron and goggles, guided the man's upper thigh across it. The saw slowed but cut nicely through the femur. Jesse's apron and goggles were splattered with bits of blood, bone, and skin. The odor of decomposing flesh filled the air. Metallica's "Harvester of Sorrow" pounded from the radio. Harley, dressed similarly to Jesse, picked up the pieces from the bench that were already cut and casually tossed them into a wheelbarrow.

Buttlicker, Jesse's huge dog, sat impatiently nearby, whining and staring at the pile of discarded meat. Harley reached inside the pile of human flesh and tossed Buttlicker the dead man's left foot. The mongrel caught it in midair and walked to a far corner where it sprawled out on the tile floor and began gnawing on the toes. Sue Ellen wandered in just as Jesse shut down the saw.

"Damn you, Jesse! I told you to bolt the fucking door," Harley bellowed.

Jesse shrugged and frowned before saying, "Sorry. I thought I did."

Harley shook his head angrily while he stomped over to the door and bolted it closed. He would have to talk with Karl once again about trusting this gal. She knew more than enough to put them all away for good, and Harley didn't like that one bit.

Sue Ellen had that bright red, post-sex, sweaty sheen to her face. She saw the wheelbarrow and walked over to it. She ran her tongue across her upper lip before slowly reaching forward and cautiously touching a piece of leg. Jesse laughed. "He ain't gonna bite ya."

"Where's his head?" She asked.

Harley, still wearing elbow-high latex gloves, started fishing around in the wheelbarrow before grunting and pulling the head, by the hair, out from underneath a pile of severed limbs. A suction-like sound let loose as the head cleared the goop. The guy's tongue was hanging out, and one eye was open and the other closed. Blood seeped and dripped from the tendons dangling from the neck.

"Ew, that's gross," Sue Ellen said while turning away.

Jesse watched Sue Ellen carefully. Although he had shot the intruder, it was Sue Ellen who had asked to slice the guy's throat when Jesse said he was going to do so. Jesse was surprised by that, and more surprised when she actually did it, as the guy begged for his life. The biggest shock was that it excited her. That was why he had left the corpse on the two-track, as Sue Ellen practically pulled his pants down in the driveway telling him to take her. He protested feebly, wondering if Karl would come back, but then she took his hand and put it down her pants. Jesse had never met a woman like her before. Sure, he liked to kill, but she seemed to really enjoy it.

Sue Ellen saw him appraising her and winked at him before turning back to Harley and asking, "What are you going to do with him?"

"Feed him to the hogs," Harley replied.

"Can I help?" She asked excitedly.

CHAPTER 7

S ue Ellen's mother was a truck-stop crack whore. A byproduct of her mother's occupation, Sue Ellen was a crack baby. Her mother aborted three prior pregnancies but finally decided to go through with the fourth. Not so much because she wanted a baby, but she instead wrongly figured her pimp, who was a mean son-of-a-bitch, would give her some time off, especially when she started showing.

Her mother died in an overdose a few weeks after giving birth to her. As the father was unknown, and Sue Ellen's mother had no known relatives that wanted anything to do with a crack baby, Baby Sue was whisked away to a foster family.

Babies were in high demand for adoption. The family that adopted baby Sue took her from her birthplace of Flint further north to the small town of McKinley. Her adoptive parents were decent people. Her father worked for the road commission and her mother worked for a couple of nearby resorts as a part-time cleaning woman.

An only child, Sue Ellen was quickly spoiled. Her adoptive parents were aware of her mother's background, including the drug usage, and were relieved that Sue Ellen didn't have any outwards signs of any problems related to her mother's drug usage during her pregnancy. At each visit to the pediatrician, Sue Ellen met or exceeded growth and development expectations.

The problems started during Sue Ellen's 13th year. Her body matured more quickly than the other girls, and she started wearing eyebrow-arching outfits to school, along with some serious makeup. The older boys quickly took notice. Sue Ellen loved the attention.

The internet was just getting popular and Sue Ellen soon discovered a vast amount of information regarding topics that would make an adult blush. She became sexually obsessed. She lost her virginity prior to her 14th birthday and soon learned that her sexuality gave her power over men, and women, that surprised her.

Simply by flirting with her English teacher, her struggling grades improved. By her senior year, she had to go a bit farther than flirting with her Calculus teacher, but she easily got an A. She relished her new power.

Her adoptive parents were appalled by her lifestyle. They were well aware of her freestyle living by the condoms they found in her purse, the various vulgar e-mails she sent and received from other students, and the numerous boys coming to their house. They sought out therapy for her when she was 17.

The closest therapist of decent repute was in Midland, Michigan. After two sessions, the therapist informed them she was displaying classic hypersexuality symptoms along with impulse control issues.

On her 18th birthday, just after graduation, Sue Ellen moved out of her house and into the trailer of her high-school Calculus teacher. His wife had just started working and they needed a live-in babysitter for their two young children. She was paid decently but made far more money for extracurricular activity from the husband that his wife wasn't aware of.

She saved up enough cash to eventually move to California, where she shared an apartment with a girlfriend from middle school. Sue Ellen had dreams of becoming a movie star.

She failed miserably after only a few commercial auditions and found employment at a seedy strip club. Despite the steady stream of drugs, men, and the LA lifestyle, she was surprised to discover she missed Northern Michigan.

After two years in LA, she returned to her hometown and quickly scooped up a job as a barmaid at the Black Bear Tavern, where she was reunited with one of her many past boyfriends, Karl Rowson. Karl and his brothers had earned a bit of a reputation as outlaws while she was away. This attracted her to him even more.

CHAPTER 8

"Dammit, Mitch, slow down! We all don't carry a badge in our pocket," Ryan complained as his speedometer read 86 in a 70mph zone.

"He's always in a hurry to get up there. I was hoping to stop at Tony's in Birch Run for breakfast, but he put a kibosh to that. He was pissed that I got in late," Troy said.

"Tony's will clog your arteries faster than drinking straight lard."

"But I love Tony's. There's nothing like them in Atlantic City. Where else do they deep-fry bacon and use 12 eggs for an omelet?"

"Like I said," Ryan replied while shaking his head.

They drove on I-75 just south of Standish. Their final destination was Oscoda County, the least populous county in Michigan's lower peninsula. Their rental cabin was in a remote forested area, just west of Mio, within the Huron National Forest, which covers over 400,000 acres.

Ryan followed Mitch as he exited busy I-75 onto the slower Highway 33 to continue north. The two-lane highway stretched straight ahead for miles through the forest like an asphalt river. The terrain was subtly changing from numerous expanses of flat farmlands to small rolling hills, predominantly pine forests, various lakes, and ponds, with small unincorporated communities in between. The plentiful pines were interspersed with oaks, beech, maples, birch, and other hardwoods. Their leaves were at peak autumn colors; various shades of gold, orange, browns, and red contrasted starkly with the dark green canvas of the pines. The sun shone brilliantly in a rare, cloudless Michigan blue sky.

"God, I miss this. It's gorgeous here," Troy exclaimed as he lowered his window and fired up a cigarette without asking Ryan. He inhaled deeply and slowly released the smoke through his nose, audibly sighing as he did so. "Please tell me you didn't forget the bud," Troy remarked.

"How could I? You only reminded me every day for the past week."

Troy laughed. "Hey, I couldn't risk flying with it. The T.S.A. still takes that shit seriously."

"Whatever, but don't let Mitch know we have it," Ryan warned.

"He needs to relax. He's not a cop up here. He's out of his jurisdiction. He could benefit from a hit or two. He wouldn't be wound up so fucking tight all the time."

"Just keep it on the downlow, bro. We don't need that drama," Ryan replied.

Troy reached down near his feet and fished out a Miller Lite from a small cooler. He extended it to Ryan, who shook his head. Troy shrugged, popped the top, and took a long gulp. "It's 12:01, bro."

"I know, but I'm waiting until we get there. One OWI arrest is enough for my lifetime," Ryan said.

"Heck, bro, that was years ago, you were only19."

"Yeah, well, once was enough for me."

"Whoa. Get off my ass!" Ryan exclaimed while glancing in his rearview mirror.

Troy swiveled around in his seat to look out the back window. An older-model, white Ford F-150 pickup, flying an

American flag from its tailgate and with a modified galvanized-pipe as a front bumper, was about two feet from their bumper. Two burly men who resembled some of the cast of *Duck Dynasty* scowled at them. "What the hell is their problem?"

"I don't know. I'm doing 15 over the speed limit. Damn rednecks!" Ryan eased off the speedometer and drifted to the right as far as he could without going off the shoulder. Despite no oncoming traffic, the truck continued tailgating them, refusing to pass. "Okay, assholes, no more Mr. Nice Guy!"

Ryan's temper was infamous among the Manning brothers. The other brothers referred to such an episode as Ryan going "full Napoleon." They reasoned it was partially due to his lack of height, red hair, and unknown insecurities, but whatever the underlying cause, a "full Napoleon" episode was not a pretty sight.

Troy, who didn't exactly have a long fuse either, attempted to calm Ryan down. "Easy, brother. We're just getting started on a relaxing week. Don't let a couple of inbreds ruin it for us."

"I didn't start this shit, and I'm trying to let them pass, but for whatever reason, they want to be jackasses. Well, they picked the wrong guy to screw with. Hang on, bro!" Ryan's voice was filled with rage.

Oh shit, he's going full Napoleon! Troy thought as he placed the can of beer in the cupholder. He flicked the cigarette out the window and braced one hand on the dash, grabbing the leather strap above the door with his other.

CHAPTER 9

"Holy crap!" Mitch exclaimed while glancing in the rearview mirror of his Suburban.

Preacher turned around in his seat just in time to see Ryan's Nissan pickup swerve three-quarters of the way off the right side of the road before braking severely. Both brothers saw a beat-up white pickup veer hard to the left, barely missing Ryan's rear bumper as it drove around it. The passenger hung half out the window, screaming something while thrusting both hands towards Ryan in a double bird salute. Ryan regained the road and rapidly accelerated towards the other pickup.

"Dear God, he's going full Napoleon," Preacher said while making the sign of the cross.

Mitch glanced forward and saw several oncoming cars. The white pickup was rapidly accelerating towards his rear. Mitch sighed. He didn't need this shit. They were supposed to be relaxing and taking a break from the stress of everyday life.

Preacher's cell phone suddenly rang. After a few seconds of listening, Preacher said to Mitch, "It's Troy. He said Ryan wants you to slow way down so we can box these idiots in, then force them to stop to have a word with them."

Mitch shook his head. "Tell him that's not going to happen. These rednecks are probably armed and nothing good will come out of it. I'm letting them pass as soon as these cars clear that are approaching. Tell him not to follow them. We're here to relax and have fun, dammit."

Preacher nodded his head in agreement and relayed the message. He then listened a few seconds and said, "Troy said Ryan's too far gone. He won't back off."

"Son of a bitch. Could he just once not fly off the handle?" Mitch replied in frustration.

The oncoming traffic cleared, and the white pickup swung to Mitch's left. He glared at the two bearded men as they passed but allowed them by without interference. Ryan's pickup was quickly approaching and began to swing left around Mitch's Suburban. Mitch abruptly veered to the left, blocking his pass attempt. Ryan's horn blared, but Mitch continued to block his maneuver to pass him. Ryan swung sharply to the right and drove half off the road, attempting to pass Mitch on the other side. Mitch mimicked his every move and slowed down his vehicle until they both eventually stopped off the side of the road.

Ryan flung himself angrily from his truck and ran up to Mitch's driver's side just as Mitch jumped out.

Oh Lord, Preacher thought as he exited the other side. *Here we go.*

Mitch put up both his hands and said, "Take it easy, brother."

Ryan yelled, "What the fuck is wrong with you? Two damn rednecks about kill me and Troy and you just let them pass?" Ryan's complexion was now redder than his hair and both his hands were balled tightly into fists.

Mitch narrowed his eyes, jabbed a finger at Ryan, and yelled back, "What do you think would have happened if I blocked them and we got them stopped? Do you think any good would have come of that? I know you're carrying, and I'm sure you have a gun for Troy as well. I guarantee you they had guns too. I just saved this trip, is what I did. I came up here to relax and have a good time with my brothers not get into a road rage incident. I deal with that type of bullshit every day."

Preacher and Troy were now standing behind Ryan. Both nodded their heads in agreement with Mitch. Ryan was breathing heavily. Preacher placed his hand gently on his shoulder and said, "Dad wouldn't want this. If he was here, he would have done exactly what Mitch did. Let it go, brother. Let's have a great week together, okay?"

Troy chimed in, "I agree. Just forget about those assholes and enjoy this week."

Ryan relaxed his hands and slowly nodded his head. "I'm sorry. You know how I can get."

The other three brothers laughed. "We sure do," Preacher said, then continued, "Now you and Mitch shake hands, and let's get up there already."

Ryan extended his hand and Mitch ignored it, stepping forward to embrace Ryan in a hug. "I love you, brother. It's all good."

"Love you too, bro," Ryan said.

Troy observed his brothers embrace with envy, wondering the last time he and Mitch even shook hands, let alone hugged.

CHAPTER 10

Karl slept until noon. He awoke to the aroma of fried bacon. Sue Ellen was already up. It had been a long night, not only of disposing a body but chopping up an entire Ford F-150 as well. The three brothers worked until 4am before calling it quits. Karl's head was throbbing from too much of Snakes's moonshine.

Massasauga, or "Snake," as Karl and his other friends referred to him, lived in a small resort near Mio. Karl met him when he did an 18-month stint in the Ionia Correctional Facility for a botched auto theft 10 years ago. Snake was half Potawatomi. His Native American ancestors once occupied the majority of the area. He was named after Michigan's only venomous snake, a type of rattlesnake, and was every bit as mean as a threatened rattler. Karl witnessed him bite another inmate's nose off in a fight.

Snake worked as a handyman at a local resort when he wasn't helping Harley out with the less legitimate aspects of his business. He had steady work, as several of the other resorts always needed repairs to the numerous rental cabins that were scattered about the area like mushrooms. His reputation for quality work at a reasonable rate kept him busy.

Karl introduced him to Harley upon his release. The two immediately hit it off. Snake became Harley's muscle when diplomatic measures failed, as they often did in criminal enterprises.

Karl, wearing only his boxers, walked into the kitchen, scratching his balls and yawning. "Somethin' smells damn good," he said.

Sue Ellen was already dressed for the day, wearing tattered, hip-hugging jeans and a black and gray flannel shirt with it tied off above her navel and enough buttons undone to properly display her cleavage. Her hair was tied off in pigtails and she was barefoot, as usual, unless working at the tavern.

Standing at the stove, she expertly flipped a pancake with the pan. A cast-iron skillet on the next burner was full of bacon from a freshly slaughtered hog. "Good morning, sunshine," she beamed, trying her best to imitate the morning news anchor on that liberal CNN station. Unfortunately, their satellite stations were limited, and Fox News was fifty-fifty at best, depending on the weather.

"Morning, babe," Karl said, He stood close behind her and leaned around her shoulder, trying to steal a kiss. She recoiled and elbowed him hard in his stomach. "Sweet Jesus, Karl, go brush your damn teeth. Your breath smells like Buttlicker's ass!"

Karl slapped her playfully on her rear, with a little more force than usual, before slumping away to the bathroom. When he returned to the kitchen a couple of minutes later, Sue Ellen told him to sit down at the table. She brought a plate full of buttermilk pancakes and thick bacon to the table. She poured him a mug of fresh ground coffee before leaning forward and kissing him. "Mmmm. Much better," she said, then poured herself a mug of coffee as well before sitting down across from him.

He smiled back at her while reaching for the maple syrup. "Where's Jesse?

"He's out checking his traps. He's hoping to have caught that huge bobcat Harley spotted a few days ago by Beaver Bridge."

"Yeah, a bobcat pelt will bring some decent coin. Even better, those Asian guys down near Toledo are offering big money for their innards. Something special about their kidneys, or liver, I cain't remember which. They dry it out and put it in some herb blend that is s'posed to give ya more sexual progress."

"Prowess," Sue Ellen corrected him.

"Huh?"

"I think you want to say 'prowess,' not 'progress,'" she said.

"What the fuck ever, Ms. College Educated," Karl said, slightly embarrassed.

"I only got one year of college. I'm not exactly a doctor, you know," she said, upset with herself for correcting him.

"Well, it's more than any of us got. Hell, Jesse barely got his GED, and Harley barely graduated. And shit, I only made it through 10th grade."

"That may be true, but you guys know the land and environment, and how to handle situations. Most of them college boys couldn't wield an ax, fix a car, butcher a deer, shoot a gun, or handle themselves in a fight. You guys are the real deal. Fuck a paper saying you got a degree. You guys got the real stuff to survive, especially when the damn Democrat socialist bastards come after us."

Karl nodded his head repeatedly in agreement. He thought back to three years prior when Sue Ellen returned to Fairview, the tiny community a few miles away. She went to work at the Black Bear Tavern, the only tavern in McKinley, as the night barmaid. In fact, besides a small family-owned motel and a fly-fishing shop, the tavern was the only business in the community.

Karl was beyond thrilled when he stopped by the tavern that fateful night for a few beers and a couple of games of pool. Karl was easily the best pool player in the county, and probably in the top 50 in the entire state. He suckered many a tourist over the years by slow-playing the first game then placing a bet on the second, and damn near running the table.

When he had reached the bar, Sue Ellen had her back to him and was bent over grabbing a couple of cold Strohs for two Steelhead fishermen. He could recognize her shapely ass anywhere. He said her name before she turned around. They hugged for a full minute across the bar.

Later that same evening in his bedroom after a raucous round of sex, they lay next to each other while she told him how her attempt to escape her small town failed miserably. He was truly sorry for her but smiled inwardly at having her back. His sex life was certainly going to improve.

For a self-described redneck, Karl wasn't a bad looking guy. At just a hair under six feet and 180 pounds, his frame was free of fat, and he had a wiry muscle tone from natural labor, not from gym weights and protein shakes. His hair was sandy brown and a bit wild. Most girls said he resembled Bradley Cooper, although with bad teeth and a crooked nose.

Despite him being able to score a lay when he needed it, the fact remained that Sue Ellen was the best-looking woman in the county, and other girls lacked her sense of adventure in the sack, not to mention her near-daily need for it. He attended highschool with Sue Ellen until he dropped out his junior year, but not before losing his virginity to her. He recalled fondly how during gym class, while on a two mile cross-country run, they snuck off the path together as the remainder of the class ran dutifully forward.

Sue Ellen practically raped him. It was over within a few seconds. She giggled at him as she ran back towards the rest of the class as he lay on his back, gym shorts and jockstrap down around his ankles. He banged her regularly after that every chance he could get. He quickly improved under her helpful tutelage. He learned she liked it rough and was surprised by a dark side of her that he would never have guessed.

"Are you listening to me, Karl?"

"Huh? Um, sure," Karl replied as she interrupted his memories.

"Sure you were," she said skeptically as he shoveled the last of the pancakes and bacon in his mouth. "I said we're running low on Oxys."

"Yeah, okay. I'll swing by Snake's place later and git some. Last time he just had Percs. Is that okay?"

"Sure, and we're still good on Adderall," she said. "You know I can't think straight without my black beauties."

"Speaking of, I sure could use some pick-me-up about now," Karl said while staring at her tits.

Sue Ellen smiled, stood slowly, and seductively unbuttoned her shirt, then started to unzip her jeans. "Why don't you show me some of that sexual prowess you were talking about earlier, baby."

The throaty growl of the gator's engine split the air as Jesse returned from checking his traps.

"Well, damn. That boy has some shitty timing, doesn't he?" Karl complained.

"Maybe not," Sue Ellen said with a half-smile.

"What?"

"Maybe he could join us, baby?" Sue Ellen said carefully, as though maybe serious and maybe not.

"What?! Are you kidding me?" Karl said, upset but just a tad bit intrigued as well.

"You know me, baby, twice the fun. If you do it for me, I'll return the favor with Jessica someday. Besides, you'll always be my main man."

Jessica was Sue Ellen's smoking hot friend that visited on occasion from LA. She dabbled in porn and whatever else she needed to do to survive there. Karl often fantasized about a threesome with her.

Jesse walked in the door and said, "Something sure smells good."

Both Karl and Sue Ellen were looking at him oddly. "What?" he asked.

CHAPTER 11

"You sure this is the right way?" Preacher asked.

"No, I'm not, but I think it is," Mitch replied as his Suburban bounced along a heavily-rutted, narrow two-track that wound through the short Jack Pines for almost a half mile off the main road.

Four big does busted through the right side of the pines just in front of them. Mitch braked hard, narrowly missing the last one as it bounded into the other side of the pines with its white tail straight up in the air. "Damn! That was close," Mitch exclaimed.

"Would have been a nice camp deer had you hit it."

"Not the way I want to harvest my venison, brother."

"I'll take any deer meat the good Lord wants to provide us in any manner he does so," Preacher countered.

"Fresh tenderloins, sautéed in onions and olive oil, with fresh garlic in a cast-iron skillet over a campfire does sound pretty damn good."

"Don't forget the morel mushrooms, brother. I froze some I found in the spring and brought 'em up," Preacher said.

"Nice, brother. You're always looking out for our stomachs as well as our souls."

They took a sharp bend to the left and a rustic one-story log cabin was just off to their right, surrounded by about an acre of cleared land. The Au Sable River flowed about 100 yards behind the cabin. The remainder of the area was surrounded by short Jack Pines. A small sign hammered to a post to the right of the entrance drive read "Whitetail Acres." A silhouette of a wood-carved buck was mounted above the sign. Mitch turned to Preacher and smiled.

Ryan nosed his truck around to the right of the Suburban and parked. The brothers gathered near Ryan's tailgate. The sweet aroma of fresh pine filled their noses. They all inhaled deeply, basking in the unseasonably warm late October sunshine. Their collective stress began to melt away.

It was their tradition to have an opening camp toast as soon as they arrived. Ryan dropped his tailgate and pulled out a Yeti cooler, handing each of them a cold bottle of Woody Wheat.

"Oh, man! I haven't had a Woody since last year," Troy said excitedly.

"Maybe you should try Viagra. After all, you boys are all seriously older than me," Ryan quipped.

"Very funny," Troy said while flipping him the bird.

Woody Wheat was a favorite of the brothers since Ryan discovered it on a fishing trip near Alpena a few years back. The small Austin Brothers microbrewery had a hit on their hands, with the hints of orange and vanilla in their delicious wheat beer.

The brothers raised their bottles and looked expectantly at Preacher.

He began, "May the good Lord bless this camp. May he provide plenty of deer sightings and greatly bless us with a clean kill when we release our arrows. We ask that he protects us from harm, as well as helps us to enjoy the splendor of his forest and the company of one other. Amen."

"Amen," the rest of them echoed as they clinked their bottles together and took generous gulps.

The brothers slipped away to unpack and claim their rooms. Preacher and Mitch had their own private bedrooms with full-size beds. Ryan and Troy shared the remaining bedroom that had two twin-beds.

The cabin was well-furnished and had a nice pantry stocked with essentials. Preacher, the unofficial cook, was happy to see a decently sized kitchen with a butcher block island. The dining room's field-stone fireplace along the far wall was the centerpiece of the cabin. Old, well-worn, but comfortable leather chairs and a sofa were arranged on either side of the fireplace. The brothers were glad to see lots of firewood stacked just outside the rear door.

"You did good, brother," Mitch said to Ryan who had rented the cabin, sight unseen, through a website.

Ryan shrugged and replied, "The photos and description told me all I needed to know. Rustic, lots of privacy, public hunting grounds all around, and the Au Sable River within 100 yards of the back door. How could I go wrong?"

"Well, if anyone is going to hunt tonight, it's already 2:30 and it'll be dark by 7. I'm going to do a quick scout of the area and set up a ground blind somewhere," Mitch stated.

"I'm with you, bro but sometime soon I'm going to break out my fly-rod and get us some trout," answered Ryan.

"I'm going to sit this hunt out. I'll get the venison chili started. I want to bake up some jalapeno cornbread too," Preacher stated.

"I'm going to help Preacher out. I'll get the campfire going as well," offered Troy.

"Suit yourselves," Mitch said. "It'll be nice to have some hot chili around a campfire when we get back. Maybe we'll have some fresh tenderloins to cook up as well. Ryan, let's camo up. I'll meet you outside in 10 minutes."

CHAPTER 12

Jesse and Karl walked out of the bedroom together in awkward silence while Sue Ellen jumped in the shower. Jesse slid over to the stove and uncovered the leftover pancakes and bacon. Sniffing each first, he piled a few pancakes on a plate and added four sticks of bacon before plopping the plate into the microwave for a quick reheat.

Karl finally broke the silence. "The pancakes were damn good. She put some pecans in 'em." When Jesse still didn't respond, Karl said, "Um, I know that was kind of weird and all. We really didn't plan it, but Sue Ellen suggested it. She's pretty, um, sexual you know," Karl said.

"It's okay. I liked it, but..." Jesse seemed to be weighing his next words carefully.

"But what? It's okay, just say whatever you're thinking."

"Well...I mean...Does that make us queer or something?"

"Oh hell no! Me and you queer, never. I mean we never kissed or even touched each other. We were giving it to Sue Ellen. Besides, in all the porno flicks, guys double-team their women all the time and they ain't queer," Karl reasoned.

"Yeah. That's true," Jesse said with obvious relief and continued, "Man, we were like a couple of rutting bucks."

Karl laughed. "I suppose we were, but just remember, this was a special situation. Sue Ellen is my woman," Karl said with a little ice in his voice, while narrowing his eyes and locking his gaze with Jesse.

Jesse quickly looked away and said, "Of course. I know that."

Karl nodded his head a few times before glancing at the wall clock. "Shit! It's 3:00 already. We got to get moving. If we don't get that Mustang for Harley today, he is gonna be pissed. Swallow, don't chew. We need to haul ass."

Jesse shoveled most of the remainder of his food in his mouth, then set the plate on the floor. Buttlicker ran over and began hungrily devouring the scraps.

A few minutes later, Karl tore out of the driveway turning left onto the dirt road. Jesse yelled, "Look out!" A newer black Chevy Suburban that was coming fast from their left braked hard and swerved to the right. Karl panicked and floored it, driving across the road before crashing into a small ditch. They both bounced hard against the dashboard as neither ever wore seat belts. Jesse's head spiderwebbed the front windshield. The Ford's horn was stuck and blowing loudly.

CHAPTER 13

Mitch and Ryan jumped from the Suburban and ran to the Explorer. The driver was leaning over and checking on his passenger. Blood ran freely from his forehead. He appeared conscious but was obviously dazed.

"Are you guys okay? Ryan asked stupidly.

"Do we fuckin' look okay?" The driver snapped back.

"I'll call 911," offered Mitch.

"Fuck that! We don't need any cops involved," the driver replied angrily.

"He needs his head looked at. He might have a concussion and need stitches," Mitch said while gesturing to the passenger.

"I'm fine," the passenger said, finally speaking but still dazed. The driver handed him a rag from the glove box to hold against his head.

"I'm calling you an ambulance just in case," Mitch said.

The driver jumped from the truck, swatted Mitch's cell phone from his hand, and stepped close to him. "The hell you are. This whole thing is your fault. You were flying. You sure you want the cops here? They'll give you a ticket. Besides, I smell beer on your breath, too."

Mitch stepped back a bit, then held his palm out to Ryan, who was balling his fists and starting towards the driver. Ryan stopped.

Mitch took a calming breath. "I was doing 45. The speed limit is 45. You pulled out of the driveway without even looking. You failed to yield, and I never struck your vehicle."

"You might not've hit us, but you caused this, and you're drunk."

"I've only had one beer. I'm well under the legal limit. If you don't want cops involved then fine, no cops, no ambulance either. As far as I'm concerned, your friend can bleed to death. And if you touch me again, I'll put you on your ass," Mitch replied with a serious edge to his voice.

The guy regarded him with a sneer and appeared to be deciding whether to fight or retreat.

Mitch was well versed in such behavior from all the arrests he had made over the years. He usually could anticipate an attack just before it happened. This guy was wound up tighter than a cheap watch and his spring was close to breaking. Mitch wasn't worried. He had the guy by two inches and at least 30 pounds. Besides, Ryan would have his back.

"Screw these tourists, Karl. We need to get going. I'm fine. I can tape this up and have Sue Ellen stitch me up later," Jesse hollered from the SUV.

Karl pointed at Mitch. "I don't care what ya say. This was your fault. If I see ya again, we'll see who puts who on his ass!"

"Whatever, Jim Bob," Mitch replied.

"My name is Karl, with a K, not Jim Bob, asshole," he said while turning and walking back to his truck. "What are you looking at, faggot?" He barked at Ryan as he passed him.

Mitch gave Ryan a warning look. Ryan showed remarkable restraint by simply saying, "Not much."

Karl jumped in the truck and saw that Jesse was resting his 44 Magnum on his thigh. "I would have popped both of those tourists, but Harley would be pissed, so I behaved. That would be a nice truck to have though."

Harley dropped the SUV into 4-wheel mode and backed out of the small ditch before gunning the engine past the two men while flipping them off.

Mitch pushed his hair back from his forehead and cursed. Ryan just shook his head before saying, "Assholes! What a way to start a trip. Two road rages in one day. What are we, redneck magnets? Maybe we should just head back to the cabin and start some serious drinking."

"Not a chance. Come on, bro. I want to find where this swampland ends. You know the big ones are in the swamp. Maybe we can hang a couple stands on the edge of it tomorrow, and I can build a ground blind deeper in."

Ryan gazed at the surrounding thick swamp and the posted warning sign and swing bar that now stood open to the driveway the rednecks had exited. "I don't know, bro. We might not want to hunt anywhere near these jackasses."

"It's public land. I'm not going to let a couple inbred, backwood rednecks scare me off," Mitch replied.

Ryan shrugged and climbed back into the Suburban. Mitch did the same after picking up his cell phone from the road.

CHAPTER 14

Troy foraged for kindling to start the campfire behind their cabin. He glanced back towards the cabin and saw Preacher busy in the kitchen. He stepped a few feet forward so that a pine tree was between him and Preacher's view, then fished out a joint from his jacket pocket. He lit it with his fancy zippo and took a hit. He exhaled with a deep sigh. The usual anxiety, guilt, and worries started to drift away. He took another hit and was seriously impressed with the quality of bud Ryan had purchased. Then, he sat on a nearby stump and reflected on his chosen profession.

The life of a professional gambler was extremely stressful. One day he was flush with cash; the next he was flat-ass broke and searching for someone to stake him in the next tournament to crawl out of the hole. He jumped on the professional gambling wagon during the peak of Texas Hold 'Em popularity. It was 2005 and he had just turned 35.

During his first two years of college at Wayne State University, he excelled as a third baseman, leading the team in stolen bases with a .305-batting average. But he was distracted by his new true love: gambling. It was a jealous lover and demanded all his attention. He lost his baseball scholarship and dropped out the first semester of his junior year.

His father was devastated. A lifelong Detroit Tiger fan, he hoped his son would one day play for them, or at least their farm team, the Toledo Mud Hens. Troy had other plans. He moved into a cheap apartment near downtown Detroit and became a regular at three casinos that recently opened in the Motor City. He scraped up gambling money by working as a business manager for a nearby small hotel chain.

He knew his skill set. It was very narrow—poker, especially No-Limit Texas Hold 'Em. He loved the strategy and odds, the percentages, the player position, reading his opponents, and everything else that made it a lot more than a game of chance. He didn't waste time at slots, roulette, or craps. He used his business knowledge from college at the card table, and, at first, was winning more than he was losing.

After several years, he had cash, girls, drugs, alcohol, and a new apartment with a view of the Detroit River. In 2006, he won a satellite tournament that landed him a seat at the World Series of Poker in Las Vegas. He finished 27th. The following year he finished 21st.

He was on a roll. With steady cash came more drugs. Cocaine was king. He loved how after just a little toot, he could play all night. Troy rolled on with his best-ever finish of 13th at the World Series of Poker in 2011. While still celebrating his victory 34 hours later with no sleep, he crashed his red Porsche 911 into the rear of a police car.

Fortunately, the officer was not inside it. Unfortunately for Troy, he was just walking towards it from a nearby diner and witnessed the crash. Troy attempted to reverse and drive away, but the officer had other plans. He pulled Troy out of the windshield of his Porsche after smashing the glass with his collapsible baton.

After a mandatory two-month rehab, a short stint in the county jail, and $25,000 in fines and attorney fees, Troy was a new and free man. He swore off cocaine but upped his intake of weed and alcohol to smooth out the daily bumps in the road. Women came and went, as did his money.

The past six months were not good. He was on a low. He hadn't been so low, for so long, ever before. Gambling always had its ups and downs, but this current down seemed bottomless. For only the third time in his gambling career, he was forced to go to a loan shark. No one wanted to stake a guy that was on a low and already behind on several payments. Like the stock market, past performance was no assurance of future earnings.

Troy almost didn't make it to the annual hunt for the first time ever. He confided his troubles to Ryan. Ryan insisted he come and even paid for his roundtrip airfare, as well as his portion of the cabin fee. Troy still wasn't sure he should go, but when rumor had it that the DiCarlo brothers were looking for him, he thought it best to get out of town for a spell.

The DiCarlo brothers specialized in delinquent loan collections. They were very skilled at their profession as several Atlantic City loan sharks utilized their services. Troy personally knew a couple of individuals that were unfortunate enough to have been paid a visit by the brothers. Ricky now walked with a permanent limp, and Chuck was missing both his pinky fingers. Despite this, they both considered themselves fortunate, as there were plenty of rumors of others disappearing.

Troy took a final drag from his joint. He was feeling as loose as a caboose, or a goose, or something like that as he stumbled back towards the firepit, carrying an armful of kindling and humming a Bob Seger tune.

• • • •

PREACHER TASTE-TESTED the cold chilli he had just emptied from his Tupperware into the cast-iron Dutch oven. He frowned, grabbed a bottle of Tabasco Sauce, and vigorously splashed several more droplets into the mixture while stirring it with a wooden spoon.

He looked out the side window to see how Troy was doing with the campfire just in time to see him stumble forward and do a face plant into the ground, his armful of kindling toppling from his grasp. Preacher ran out the rear door of the cabin. Troy stood shakily and brushed down the front of his shirt and pants. "I'm fine. All good," he said with slurred speech as Preacher approached.

"Brother, you need to slow down. You won't make it until dark if you keep up this pace," Preacher scolded gently.

"I'm fine, mother. I'm fine," Troy replied with a stupid smile.

"Do you need a hand with the fire? I'm going to heat the chili over it once you get it going."

"Nope. I got it covered, bro. Could you maybe bring me another Woody please?"

Preacher smiled and shook his head. Best to pick his battles. It was only the first day. If Troy wanted to pass out before dark, he wouldn't stand in his way. "Sure thing, brother. Just don't fall into the fire."

Troy saluted him and began picking up the scattered kindling. He was sure glad Preacher witnessed his fall and not Mitch. *Fucking Mitch needs to chill*, thought Troy.

CHAPTER 15

Mitch drove about three quarters of a mile down the road when the thick swamp finally ended. It was bordered by a tall stand of white and red oak trees interspersed with an occasional tall pine. Mitch continued forward another hundred yards before spotting a faint two-track that snaked through the oaks.

"Let's check it out," he said to Ryan, who nodded in agreement.

An hour later, Mitch was nestled into a dirt depression caused by the toppling of a huge white pine, probably from a wind shear from one of the many summer storms. His back was protected by the giant root structure of the fallen tree. He used his folding handsaw to trim some other low hanging branches from nearby trees to conceal his sides. He left an opening facing the heavily traveled deer run he had walked in on. Any deer moseying down the trail would offer an easy 25-yard shot.

Mitch sat comfortably on a small folding camo chair with a nylon seat. He was a good half mile back in the swamp from the oak-lined edge they drove into. It was tough terrain interspersed with spongy, soggy moss-covered ground, but after about a quarter mile in he discovered a well-worn primary deer run, commonly referred to as a "cow path." He followed it several hundred yards farther in until it converged with two other lesser trails. Satisfied with the spot, he looked around and spied the deadfall. He wasn't too concerned about leaving behind human scent as he had on rubber boots and ScentLok camouflage coveralls.

He finally began to unwind. The past week at work was crazy busy. His second ex-wife, Tonia, was starting her shit again about needing more child support. Luckily, his first marriage was over before they had any children. It lasted 18 months. His second lasted twice that long and his only child, a daughter they named Katie, now 10, was the love of his life. Despite Tonia having a full-time job as an emergency room nurse, and having hired a great lawyer for the divorce, she was always wanting more.

At least Tonia didn't give him a hard time regarding his visitation with Katie. He had her every other weekend, and for a full month each summer, and was happy to take her anytime other time he wasn't working. She was already showing an interest in hunting which irked Tonia to no end.

Mitch admired his new Mission compound bow by Matthews resting on his lap. It wasn't a high-dollar bow, but it had 80 percent let-off and was set at 75 pounds, plenty of power to take down any deer. Mitch had reluctantly retired his XI Legend Magnum after 14 years of use. The company was now defunct, but the old bow had served him well, accounting for 11 deer, including seven nice bucks.

Mitch was good at sitting still and remained nearly motionless. The first 90 minutes passed by quickly. He was tormented by a fat gray fox squirrel that chattered at him incessantly, like his ex-wives, for the first half hour before finally losing interest and moving onward. *Also just like my ex-wives*, he thought wryly. A flock of small wrens fluttered about his blind a few minutes later. One of them almost landed on his head before quickly changing its flight path.

After that, no other critters visited, besides the occasional hawk circling the air currents high above him. The damp, musty earth smell of the swamp filled his nostrils. Dusk was rapidly settling in as the night shift of the forest began to stir. An owl hooted softly as a raccoon scurried down from a nearby tree, and a small bat darted erratically through the trees. Mitch felt the first cool waves of thermal air settling in from above, displacing the warmer air from earlier in the day.

It was finally prime time! Like the two minute warning in a football game, the final half hour shooting light was usually the most productive of the entire late afternoon hunt. The deer would start moving in earnest in search of their dinner, hopefully passing his way.

Not long after, Mitch heard a shuffling noise to his right-rear. He grasped his bow a bit tighter and closed his eyes to focus entirely on the noise. He heard it again. Something was coming his way and was getting close. The hesitant nature suggested the wary white-tail deer. His heartbeat accelerated as he pictured a huge swamp buck approaching. He would shoot a doe, as he had a combo-license that allowed two deer to be taken, and he was out of venison meat, but he preferred a big buck.

Darkness was settling in fast, like a black fog, He willed the deer to hurry forward. The wind was in his favor so it shouldn't have winded him, and it certainly couldn't see him. A stillness and eerie quietness, not unlike in a library, settled in, as it often did in the wild just before dark. Mitch swore he could hear his own heart beating.

Unexpectedly, an ear-piercing howl shattered the dead quiet swamp, scaring the bejesus out of Mitch. He didn't startle easy but the suddenness and closeness of it was unnerving. He never heard anything like it in over 30 years of deer hunting. He practically tossed his bow to the ground as he swiftly drew his Smith & Wesson .40 caliber pistol from his waistband, standing and turning around to see what the hell was behind him.

About 35 yards away he glimpsed a dark figure moving quickly away at a diagonal from his blind. His first thought was a black bear, but that didn't seem quite right because it appeared to be walking upright. Whatever it was, he was damn glad it was moving away from him. He hadn't realized he was tracking it with his pistol sights. It quickly disappeared into the shadows and thick undergrowth.

He let out a long slow breath he wasn't aware he had been holding and was suddenly seized with an adrenaline dump as his hands began to tremble. *Screw this!* He thought as he grabbed his bow and reluctantly tucked his pistol back into his waistband to hold onto his flashlight.

He practically jogged out of the swamp, turning around frequently and scanning behind him with his flashlight, its beam bouncing off trees and shrubs. For a brief second, each one resembled the figure he had just seen. Coyotes began to yip all around him, but he hardly noticed as the incredibly strange howl seemed to still fill his ears. "Get a grip, Mitch," he whispered to himself as he continued forward to the safety of his Suburban.

Ryan had elected to hunt the edge of the oaks, just a couple hundred yards from the Suburban. He was standing outside the SUV sipping a cold Woody Wheat when he saw Mitch's flashlight beam bouncing around. Mitch emerged from the edge of the swamp 50 feet away at a jog and was nervously looking over his shoulder.

"You okay, bro?" Ryan asked.

"I'm good, but there is something freaky back there. It wigged me out."

Ryan could tell Mitch was unsettled. "What was it?"

"Not sure, but it was big, and it screamed at me! I about pissed myself."

"Bigfoot?" Ryan asked, half in jest.

"I don't know, brother, it was too dark, and I only caught a few quick glimpses of it. I'm thinking a black bear, but damn I never heard a sound as it made before. It was straight out of a horror movie."

"Well, tomorrow we can check it out in the daylight, maybe see some tracks or something. Man, I love those Bigfoot shows. Who knows, maybe you saw one."

"Ryan, I don't think it was that big. It seemed almost human size, like maybe 6 feet or so. Like an upright black bear."

"Go ahead, bro, be a doubter, but I believe."

"We'll check it out tomorrow after daylight. I'm not going back there in the morning before daybreak, that is for damn sure," Mitch replied.

CHAPTER 16

The Dogman Den was Alpena's newest microbrewery. The business was located just southwest of city limits, nestled in a patch of tall pines alongside Mud Lake. Resembling a rustic lodge, its twin dormers protruded from either side of the main entrance, and it boasted a front porch complete with twenty rocking chairs lined up, just like at Cracker Barrel. The dark stained logs were capped with a forest green corrugated metal roof. Its best feature was a huge deck jutting off the back with a spectacular view of the lake.

The owner was apparently doing quite well, as his classic 1968 Shelby GT Ford Mustang was parked in the side lot. Karl and Jesse waited patiently until dark. They had parked the Explorer in the driveway of an unoccupied cabin about a quarter mile down the street. The lake was mostly empty this late in the fall. The cabins were mainly summertime retreats for well-to-do residents from the lower portion of the state or neighboring Ohio.

The Shelby was parked next to the brewery under an extremely bright overhead pole lamp. As it was Friday night, the lot was half full, despite it being the offseason.

Jesse took careful aim with his sling-shot from the edge of the pines that bordered the parking lot and expertly shot the light out on his first attempt. They spotted surveillance cameras as soon as they walked up through the trees, one of which was focused directly on the car. Harley had warned them not to drive into the lot as there were several cameras and the police would certainly later review the footage. As an extra precaution, both wore full camouflage outfits as well as camo ny-lon face shields with ball caps. No way could they be identi-fied even if captured on camera. Each also wore thin black latex gloves.

After patiently waiting several more minutes, with no one coming or going, Karl gave Jesse the thumbs up. Jesse nodded once then ran in a half-crouched position to the driver's side of the car. He tried the door handle but, as expected, it was locked; also as expected, no alarm activated. If it had, he would have aborted, but Harley's source, a dishwasher at the establish-ment, told him it wasn't alarmed.

Jesse used a quick pick to pop the lock and was inside the car in 10 seconds.

Karl could no longer see him as he bent over, working the ignition wires underneath the dash. *Come on,* Karl thought to himself after several more seconds elapsed.

"Oh shit, shit, no!" Karl mumbled to himself as a county sheriff car slowly turned into the driveway from the main road. The low beams from the car panned across the side parking lot as it pulled into the parking space directly adjacent to the Shel-by.

Karl nearly went into cardiac arrest. The police car's engine shut down just as the Shelby's throaty engine roared to life. The lone deputy was partially out of his car and appeared star-tled by the car firing up. Little did Karl, or Jesse, know at the time that the deputy was a friend of the car's owner and as such knew the owner would never allow anyone else to drive it. The deputy bent low to see inside the darkened passenger window while making a motion for the occupant to roll down the win-dow.

Jesse slammed the gearshift into reverse and squealed the Shelby's tires. He expertly J-turned behind the deputy's car before dropping it into first and popping the clutch. The Shelby smoked its tire for a couple of seconds until finally gaining traction and rocketing forward, just as a man and woman walking hand-in-hand stepped into his path from the main porch.

Karl watched, wide-eyed, as Jesse fishtailed wildly around the couple, narrowly missing them before speeding forward and power-sliding onto the main road. The deputy jumped into his squad car and reversed out almost as wildly. The overhead alternating, flashing strobes of blue and red now activated.

Karl swore under his breath while raising his .22, opensite rifle to his shoulder and leaned against a pine to steady his aim. He depressed the trigger quickly in succession three times. The squad car turned left into the driveway heading toward the main road but rolled to a stop just before reaching it, as both back tires were now flat.

The angry deputy hopped from his car to determine what happened. The couple that had almost been hit by the car frantically pointed towards the tree line Karl was concealed in, yelling that they saw muzzle flashes and heard gunshots from that way.

"Fuck me!" Karl hissed to himself as he turned and fled headlong through the pines as fast as he could in the dark. Fortunately, he had a 50-yard head start; unfortunately, the deputy had a canine in the back of his cruiser. The deputy hit the remote switch to the rear car door and his German Shepherd, Buzz Kill, jumped out. The deputy pointed and yelled "geh und hol ihn," a German command meaning, go get him!

Karl only smoked five to six cigarettes a day, but his lungs were on fire after only a hundred yards, and he had 350 to go before reaching his SUV. He didn't hear the deputy pursuing him but knew he was calling for backup. Fortunately, that normally meant 20 to 30 minutes at the minimum in the north country.

Karl went another 50 yards and forced himself to stop, breathing heavily as he tried to listen for approaching footsteps. As he peered over his shoulder, straining to see through the darkness, he sensed something approaching fast. Before he could react a black shadow exploded through a small patch of weeds and hurtled towards him.

He instinctively ducked and rolled forward as something bit through his rear jacket collar near the bottom of his neck. Luckily, it had latched onto the rolled-up hood instead of his flesh. As he tried to stand, the dog frantically held on and pulled backward on the collar. Like a hockey player pulling the opposing player's jersey over his head, the dog was winning the battle. Karl fired the rifle blindly while thrusting it forward.

The round took a chunk out of the canine's right ear. The dog yelped and released its grasp. Karl stood and shrugged his jacket down and batted the dog's face away with the rifle butt just as it launched at him again. The dog was momentarily knocked away but circled back towards him while growling menacingly.

Karl raised his .22 to his shoulder and aimed at the dog's head just as a sharp whistle pierced the air. Buzz Kill immediately wheeled around and ran back towards its handler. Three pistol shots rang out in quick succession from at least 30 yards back. One round zinged by his ear like an angry hornet.

"If you hurt my dog, I'll kill you! You hear me? I will fucking kill you!" The deputy's frustrated and angry voice bellowed.

Karl started jogging again, crouching low as he did so. He finally saw the silhouette of his SUV ahead. He heard a twig snap about 30 yards behind him. Was that trigger-happy deputy still following him? Shooting out his tires and at his dog was one thing, but he sure as hell didn't want to shoot a deputy. That would bring a shitload of cops to the area for a long time. Besides, Harley would go ballistic.

Karl yanked open the driver's side door, tossed the rifle onto the passenger seat, and nervously fumbled for his keys. Just as the engine cranked over his passenger side window exploded and a bullet nicked his nose before lodging into the metal frame of his side window. Karl swore then yanked the gear selector to drive and floored it. As he was just about to turn onto the main road, his rear windshield exploded as two more bullets entered. One lodged in the passenger side rear headrest while the other continued out through the front windshield, leaving behind a perfect hole to accompany the earlier damage from Jesse's forehead.

Karl swore again as he practically rolled the SUV onto its side while turning too fast onto the main road. He flew away from the scene with his heart hammering as fast as the pistons in the Ford's engine.

CHAPTER 17

The four Manning brothers sat around a roaring campfire, enjoying Preacher's venison chili, jalapeno cornbread, and ice-cold Woodys. Mitch had just recounted what had happened earlier in the woods to his other two brothers.

"It sounds like a black bear to me. I've seen them walk upright before," Preacher said.

"Walk maybe, but run?" Troy countered.

"I'm telling you guys, it was a Bigfoot sighting," Ryan said with authority.

"I don't know what it was, but it wasn't human, that's for damn sure. I've never heard anything scream like that," Mitch replied, then took another bite of chili. "This is fantastic, Preacher. Not too hot but still spicy." Ryan and Troy grunted their agreement,

Preacher gazed upwards at the crescent moon and a cloudless, inky-black sky dotted with stars. Coyotes yipped and howled far off. He sipped his beer and announced, "It doesn't get any better than this, boys. Fresh, northern pollution-free, pine-scented air, free-range, hormone-free, personally harvested venison chili, heated over an outdoor campfire, drinking a cold beer with my brothers amidst God's splendor."

"Amen to that!" Mitch replied.

"Well said, Preacher. You should have plenty of material after this week for a sermon or two," Ryan offered.

"You get to say sermons? I thought that was just for the actual priest," Troy asked.

"Well, if you went to church more than at Christmas and Easter, you would know that deacons say sermons occasionally as well," Preached replied.

"To be honest, I think I missed Easter," Troy answered.

Preacher shook his head. "Mom and Dad raised you better than that, Troy."

"I've been busy," Troy offered.

"Seriously? Too busy for your Creator?"

Mitch and Ryan exchanged furtive glances from across the fire. If Preacher continued on his course, Troy would blow. It happened every camp, but not usually until near the end.

Mitch didn't respect Troy's attitude, but he wanted them all to get along. "Anyone need another beer?" He asked while reaching in the cooler behind him, hoping to veer the conversation down a different road.

Ryan raised his hand. Troy downed his last few ounces then tossed the bottle into the flames and raised his hand as well. Mitch pitched each of them a bottle. Ryan juggled it while Troy easily caught his in one hand. His baseball days were long behind but his instincts were still sharp.

"Preacher?" Mitch asked.

"Why not. It's deer camp after all," he answered. After taking his bottle from Mitch, he twisted off the cap, took a deep pull, then asked, "So what's the game plan tomorrow?"

A log in the fire popped, showering sparks upwards. "Ryan and I are waiting for first light before heading out to my blind. We want to look for tracks to determine what I saw," Mitch replied. "Besides, I could use help hauling back my tree stand and climbing sticks. It's super thick there. No way I'm ground hunting back there. Nothing is going to sneak up on my six again."

Preacher, who was scared shitless of bears but would never admit it, said, "Better to be cautious for sure. Twenty feet above ground is always safer than on the ground. I think I'll sleep in and get breakfast ready for when you guys come back. I'm thinking biscuits and gravy with venison sausage links and home fries."

"It doesn't sound like anyone is hunting tomorrow morning. What the heck. I suppose I'll do some walking and stalking at first light around the area. Maybe I'll get a shot opportunity. Someone's gotta hunt!"

"Good deal. It sounds like we have solid plans for the morning. Anyone want to claim dinner for tomorrow night?" Preacher asked.

"I'm calling bar night. Let's have a nice greasy burger, or wings, and fries. We passed a place called the Black Bear Tavern a few miles back. It looked like just the spot for our needs," Ryan replied.

"I'm good with that," Troy quickly piped up. He was never one to pass up an opportunity to visit a bar, tavern, or other watering hole.

"Sounds okay to me, but remember what happened last year at bar night," Mitch said, his tone turning serious.

Preacher, Mitch, and Ryan all looked at Troy.

"What? It was no big deal," Troy replied.

"I guess that depends on your definition of 'no big deal.' Having the police called on us seems like kind of a big deal to me." Preacher admonished.

"Mitch smoothed it out. It was just a misunderstanding," Troy replied.

"Just make sure we don't have a repeat performance," Mitch said.

"You guys need to relax. Jeesh. I'm single after all. How was I supposed to know she was married? Besides, she was all over me. What was I supposed to do?" Troy reasoned.

"Banging her in my truck was probably not the best idea, especially with her husband in the bar!" Ryan answered.

"In retrospect, I suppose it wasn't, but once again, I didn't know she was married," Troy lied.

Preacher and Mitch shook their heads.

A shooting star streaked across the dark sky from east to west with a long trail of fire.

"Holy shit, did you see that?!" Troy exclaimed.

Mitch and Ryan did but Preacher missed it.

Feeling buzzed from his earlier joint and multiple beers, Troy said with slurred speech, "I love you guys. I really do. There isn't anything I wouldn't do for you. I would lay down my life for any of you."

"Me too, bro," Ryan said. Preacher nodded his head. Mitch just stared into the fire and remained silent.

CHAPTER 18

Jesse stashed the stolen Shelby about a mile away from their home down a little-used two-track. He drove it about 200 yards off the road then parked it between several shrubs. His head was pounding with a headache from the earlier collision with Karl's front windshield. He surely had what all those football players got when they were tackled too hard. What was it called? A concussion? Yeah, that was it, a concussion, he thought. At least the bleeding had stopped, thanks to a large piece of hastily applied silver duct tape.

He hopped out of the car and quickly removed the license plate. He would be back before first light to retrieve it. Harley liked them to leave the stolen cars somewhere else overnight to cool down. It was unlikely anyone would find it in the next 10 hours as not too many folks were driving on barely-noticeable two-tracks in the dark. However, in the unlikely event that someone had followed Jesse, at least he would not lead them directly to their home.

Jesse hiked back to the main road and started walking. He was about halfway home when Karl's Explorer approached and stopped adjacent to him. Jesse climbed in and noticed the bullet-hole in the front windshield next to his earlier head impression. "Motherfucker almost killed me!" Karl said excitedly.

"What happened to your nose?" Jesse asked after noticing the end was wrapped up with a wad of duct tape.

"The damn pig shot at my ass and my ride! One of his bullets clipped my nose."

Jesse laughed.

"That's funny to you?"

"Naw, I was just thinking he must have been a piss-poor shot if he was shooting at your ass and hit your nose," Jesse said, laughing some more.

"It was metaphysically speaking, dickhead," Karl said.

Jesse didn't think that "metaphysically" was the correct word but wasn't sure, so he didn't correct Karl. Hell, it had five syllables; any word with more than two was a challenge for either of them. Jesse wondered why the exhaust sounded so loud and looked around, thinking a rear window was down, when he noticed the back windshield was shattered.

"The deputy had a dog, too. He sent the son-of-a-bitch after me."

"You didn't hurt the dog, did ya?"

"Hell yes, I did. I shot the bitch and smacked it upside its head with my rifle butt. The crazy thing was trying to eat me alive!"

"Ah, man. It was just doing what it's trained to do. You shouldn't have shot the dog."

"Relax about the fucking dog. It ran off just fine. I think I just nicked it like the cop did my nose. Maybe I shouldn't have shot the tires out of the cop's car neither. You think the guy just magically stopped chasing ya?"

"I would have outrun him no problem. It's a bitchin' car. I was driving that fucker like Vin Diesel does in Fast and Furious. What happened to the cop? Did you shoot him too?"

"No way. I'm not as fucked up in the head as you. Besides, Harley would have killed me if I did."

"Probably true," Jesse conceded.

They pulled into their driveway and stopped inches from the gate. "It ain't gonna open itself," Karl stated while looking expectantly at Jesse.

Jesse jumped from the SUV and unlocked the gate, swinging it inward. Karl drove in and waited for Jesse to re-lock it. They then continued up the driveway toward their home.

"What the hell happened to you two?!" Harley asked as Jesse and Karl walked into the living room. He was seated in the La-Z-Boy, drinking a Busch light and watching Dancing With The Stars.

"It's been a bad fuckin' day!" Karl replied as he walked to his bedroom to get some Oxies for him and Jesse.

Jesse walked into the kitchen to grab a couple of beers.

"Did you get the car?" Harley asked while admiring the professional dancers' long, shapely legs.

Jesse returned with two cans of beer and popped one open. He took a long swallow before stating, "We got it. It's a bitchin' car. Do we have to part it out?"

"Yeah we do. Whatcha think, we can just paint it a different color and you can drive it around and no one will be suspicious?"

"I guess not."

Karl walked back in, handed Jesse a couple of Oxys, and said, "For your pain, bro." Jesse handed him the other beer.

Harley watched them as they washed the Oxys down with beer. "Okay, now tell me what the fuck happened. You two look even uglier than usual with all that duct tape on your faces."

Karl told him everything, starting with the accident coming out of their driveway, and nearly being killed by the trigger-happy deputy.

"Holy shit! You two did have a bad day."

"It wasn't all bad, it started out pretty damn good," Jesse said, recalling the threesome with Sue Ellen.

"Why what happened this morning?" Harley asked curiously.

Karl shot Jesse a warning look and interjected, "He had a good morning on his trap line."

Harley looked at Karl, then Jesse, and said, "Good deal. Did you get that big bobcat?"

"Naw, not yet, but I did get a coyote and three snowshoe hares."

"Nice. Karl, I reckon you realize we're gonna have to chop and bury your Ford, especially since the deputy saw it," Harley said, then drained his beer and belched loudly.

"I knows it. Pisses me off, though. It's been a great fucking ride."

"We'll get you something else. Don't sweat it. Jesse, go park it in the barn. We don't want to take any chances of someone spotting it in the off chance you were followed," Karl ordered.

"Ain't no one followed us, Harley," he replied.

"Just do it, dickhead," Karl said.

Jesse glared at Karl then stomped out of the house. Harley fired up a joint, took a hit, and offered it to Karl. He took an extended hit, coughed twice, then passed it back.

"I'll be in the shop early tomorrow. Snake's cousin is going to take some parts down to Cincinnati. I want him on the road by seven. Make sure you get the Shelby in the barn before first light. I'll wake you when I leave." Harley instructed.

"Will do, and we'll get started on my truck first thing. Um, I need to borrow your wrecker in a few hours to pick up Sue Ellen from work," Karl said.

"Naw you don't. She's out in the barn doing her pole workout or whatever she does on that thing. Larry sent her home early since it was slow."

"Oh. Well, cool. Maybe I better go check on her," Karl said and stood up.

"Relax. She's fine. Jesse's out there too, remember." Harley said.

Karl did remember and wanted to check on her all the more, but Harley said, "Grab us a couple more beers and relax. Check out these chicks, they're smokin' hot." He gestured at the dancers on the 48" TV.

CHAPTER 19

It was a half-hour before sunup. Ryan and Mitch sipped coffee at the kitchen table, each nursing a slight hangover. Troy had left the cabin a few minutes earlier to stalk the immediate area with his crossbow. Preacher was sleeping soundly.

Ryan moaned and rubbed his forehead. "I was fine until Troy opened the bottle of Buffalo Chase," he complained.

"Well, at least it wasn't Jack Daniels. That stuff always kicks my ass," Mitch chimed in and added, "You weren't too bad in both Hold 'Em games last night. Troy isn't used to getting beat by us lowly amateurs."

"True that, brother. He wasn't too happy when he thought he had me with his full house and I had the straight flush."

"No. He sure wasn't." Mitch said with a grin.

"So, what's the game plan this morning?" Ryan asked.

Mitch grabbed a homemade chocolate chip cookie from a plate of them that Ryan's fiancée, Frankie, had made and took a bite. He chewed thoughtfully before saying, "We'll carry my stand and ladder sticks back to my ground blind and set that up for the evening hunt, then look around for some tracks to determine what that thing was. There's plenty of good deer runs around if you want to set up in the same area, bro. To be honest, I wouldn't mind some back-up if that thing comes back."

"I was thinking the same thing, brother. I'll bring my lightweight climbing stand. If I see a good spot, I'll set up nearby and if it produces tonight, hang my other stand there tomorrow."

"Sounds good. Tell Frankie these cookies are awesome." Mitch looked at his watch before saying, "It's time to camo-up bro. Departure time in 10 minutes."

Ryan, oblivious to what Mitch had just said, intently studied a small map of the area he had picked up yesterday at a ranger station on the way in. "Earth to Ryan," Mitch said.

"What's a dogman?" Ryan asked without looking up from his map.

"A dog what?"

"A dogman," Ryan repeated while jabbing his index finger at the map. "The name of the swamp we're hunting is called Dogman Swamp!"

Mitch stood and walked around the table to lean over Ryan's shoulder. "Huh. I don't know."

Ryan was already trying to Google it, but the connectivity was poor, and nothing loaded. He swore. "Well, maybe that's what you saw last night. A dogman."

"Whatever it was, it didn't bark like a dog, bro, and it walked upright. Do dogs do that?"

"No, but a dogman might," Ryan reasoned.

"When we head to the bar tonight, we can ask a local what it is. I'm sure they'll know. But for now, I'm heading out. Once we get our stands hung, we can do a little two-track scouting and see what's moving in the area, but we need to scoot. Sun-up is soon."

Fifteen minutes later, as the sun was rising, they were driving toward their two-track from the night before when a Shelby Ford Mustang pulled slowly out of the woods 50 yards ahead. It turned left onto the main road, now heading towards them.

"Sweet car!" Ryan exclaimed.

"Sure is, but kind of strange to be driving it out of a forest just after sunrise." The cop in Mitch reasoned aloud.

Both of them looked at the occupants as it passed by. The passenger had his head turned to the right and the driver looked straight ahead, neither showing the slightest interest in the only other vehicle on the road. *Guilty behavior for sure,* Mitch thought, just like when he rolled by someone in his police car who had a suspended license or drugs in their car. The guilty never wanted to make eye contact. His suspicions were further confirmed when he noted in his side mirror the Shelby didn't have a license plate attached to the rear bumper.

"I think that was the same two bozos from yesterday that we almost hit," Ryan exclaimed.

"I'm certain of it, just as I am that they're driving a stolen car now," answered Mitch, who watched the car intently in his rear-view mirror until it disappeared.

"We gonna follow them?"

"Nah. I'm off duty and out of my jurisdiction, bro. Besides, we know where they're headed. I'll call the local law and give them a heads up on what we saw," Mitch answered as he turned onto the two-track and stopped. He fished his cell phone from his jacket pocket and saw he had no service. Ryan did the same and got the same results. "I'll call 'em later when we get somewhere with a decent signal. I came here to relax, not fucking work," Mitch complained.

"You think they recognized us?" Ryan asked.

"They sure as hell recognized the Suburban, bro. Not too many newer black Suburbans cruising this neighborhood," Mitch reasoned.

"Sorry. That was a stupid question. Do you think we should be concerned about them coming back to look for us?"

"Nah. I doubt it. We don't know for sure it's even stolen," Mitch answered, but his cop senses were telling him otherwise. "Just make sure you gun-up before we head into the swamp, just in case."

Ryan lifted his jacket to reveal his pistol tucked into his waistband. "Way ahead of you, bro. I'm not going into dogman territory with just a bow."

Mitch laughed and they fist-bumped as he continued down the lane.

CHAPTER 20

"It's those same assholes from yesterday," Jesse exclaimed after turning the Shelby off the two-track onto the main dirt road and seeing the approaching black Suburban.

"Just keep driving. Don't make eye contact, act normal," Karl said while looking to his right to obscure his face. As the Suburban drove by, they could feel the eyes of the occupants all over them.

"This ain't good, Karl. We need to do something."

"Relax and just keep going. If they turn around we'll do what we gots to do," Karl replied while taking his revolver out of his rear waistband and resting it on his thigh. "Did they turn around or stop?"

Jesse's eyes were locked on the rearview mirror. "Nope, still going forward."

Karl released a breath he didn't know he was holding and said, "Okay, good. Keep an eye on that mirror. If you don't see 'em following us, just turn in our driveway as planned."

"Then what?" Jesse inquired.

"Then we start taking apart my Explorer as Harley told us to."

Jesse shook his head and said, "I know those guys saw us."

"'Course they did, but that doesn't mean they recognized us, and so what if they did? They're just a couple of tourists. They don't know this car ain't ours." Karl reasoned.

Jesse was still shaking his head. "We better call Harley and see what he thinks."

"We ain't fucking bothering Harley about this. He already doesn't think we're smart enough to figure things out on our own," Karl said with an authoritative tone.

"That's 'cause we ain't."

"Speak for yourself, dickhead. I'm smart enough for both of us."

Jesse turned into their driveway after triple-checking his rearview mirror. He was seething inwardly. He hated being called names, especially by his brother. He was expelled from school numerous times for fighting as he was often bullied because he was an odd child. The other kids nicknamed him "Inbred." He never fought Karl, except for roughhousing, but secretly often fantasied about kicking his ass.

He was pretty sure he could. Harley taught them both how to fight. Harley had learned to hone his street-fighting to high art during his five-year prison stint, over 20 years ago, after being caught by a Michigan State Police Task Force targeting stolen cars from the Detroit area. Harley often boasted how he was the enforcer among his prison gang.

He told them he had handled all beefs with the other gangs and handled them well. During their early training sessions, Karl easily bested him, but Jesse was only 15 then. He was much stronger and faster now. Jesse smiled inwardly knowing that one day soon he would show Karl who was second in command, and it wasn't going to be decided by age.

Jesse stopped the Shelby in front of the second bay door, waiting for Karl to open it. He then pulled the Shelby inside as Karl hauled the corrugated-metal, windowless door down, and bolted it shut. He jumped out of the car and heard country music from the far side of the barn. Keith Urban was singing something about a John Deere.

Sue Ellen walked through a connecting interior door. A light sheen of sweat covered her body as she had just finished a pole workout. She was wearing black spandex yoga pants and a pink sports bra. "Morning, boys," she purred.

Jesse's eyes undressed her. His prior thoughts of rage against Karl were now replaced with more carnal desires.

"Now that's a sweet ride," Sue Ellen exclaimed as she strode past the guys over to the Shelby. She ran her fingertips gently over the curves of the hood as though stroking a lover. She looked back at Karl and said, "Take me for a ride in this beast."

"No can do!" Karl replied while shaking his head.

"Oh, come on! Before you carve this beauty up, you gotta give me a ride in it," she begged.

"No way, Sue Ellen. Harley would kill me. Someone could spot us." Karl replied without mentioning they were already spotted by someone.

Sue Ellen pushed out her lower lip and did her best pouty face. "You're no fun!" She sauntered past them and grabbed Jesse's ass as she passed, making certain Karl saw she did it. When she entered her workout room, she slammed the door behind her.

"Crazy woman," Karl mumbled to himself. "I could use a coffee before we get started. You get the tools ready, and I'll grab us a couple of brews from the house." Jesse nodded his head and walked over to the tool shelf.

A few minutes later, Karl was walking down the front porch steps of the cabin carrying two mugs of coffee when he heard the growl of the Shelby's engine roar to life. As he stepped into the driveway, it came roaring towards him from the barn. *What the fuck?!* He thought as it slid to a stop next to him.

Sue Ellen was seated in the passenger seat with the window down, smiling wickedly at him. Jesse leaned forward from his seat and said, "We'll be back in a couple hours, dickhead. You can get started on your Explorer without me." Jesse mashed the accelerator to the floor, showering Karl with dirt and stones.

Karl watched dumbfounded as the Shelby raced down the driveway, disappearing from his sight. His anger was greater than he ever remembered. He tossed the coffee mugs to the ground and sprinted into the garage intending to give chase, but saw his Explorer now had four flat tires.

"Fuck, fuck, fuck!" He bellowed. *Jesse's dead. A half-brother or not, the boy is dead!* Karl thought. He grabbed a hammer from the workbench and hurled it through his Explorer's front window.

CHAPTER 21

The dawn's darkness was fading fast as the western horizon revealed a golden hue. Troy stalked the edge of the Au Sable that flowed behind their cabin. The thousands of jack pines bordering each side of it thinned out considerably about 30 feet from the edge of its banks. There was plenty of spongy moss in which to place his deliberate steps. He walked with the gentle east wind in his face so as to not allow the deer to scent him. Despite his experience and knowledge, he had not harvested a deer, buck or doe, in the last five hunting seasons. He was hoping to end that drought this year.

Troy froze in place upon glimpsing movement 30 yards ahead to his left in the short pines. Whatever the brief flash of tan was, it was moving towards the water and would exit the pines soon. Troy ever so slowly raised his Hoyt compound bow and came smoothly to full draw. The 75-pound initial bow had an 80% let-off, allowing him to easily hold the bow at full draw while waiting for the animal to offer a shot.

A red fox cautiously stepped into view. It glanced in Troy's direction, but he remained completely still. His camo outfit did the trick as the fox looked to its left then headed away from Troy, paralleling the little river's bank with its long bushy tail dragging behind it. Troy lowered his bow, smiling to himself at sighting such a cool critter, especially with it being completely unaware of his presence. Now, if only a deer would appear.

Troy rested his bow on the ground and plopped down along the riverbank. He fished out a cigarette and fired it up with a gold-plated Zippo he won two years earlier from some

86

semi-famous rapper during a celebrity poker game. It had tiny diamond horseshoe on each side. The rapper claimed it cost him $10,000 to custom design. Troy took a heavy drag on his cigarette and stashed the lighter deep in his pocket. He was hoping it would prove to be a good luck charm for him but thus far it was anything but. He would have to pawn it soon if things didn't get better.

He couldn't believe that his little brother not only beat him once but twice the prior night in Texas Hold 'Em. It wasn't like he expected to win every game but, damn, if he couldn't beat his amateur brothers, how could he expect to win a big tournament against other professionals? In retrospect, he *had* been half-high and full drunk last night.

He finished the cigarette, admiring the fast-flowing river one last time before flicking the butt into it. He wasn't one to litter, but he sure as hell didn't want to start a forest fire. He figured the river was a safer choice for disposal than the dry, pine-needle covered ground. He watched the butt quickly float away then returned his gaze in front of him. His heart stopped, as did time.

A huge-bodied buck sporting a 12-point wide rack was staring at him from across the river, half concealed inside the jack pines.

Troy felt his heart restart and it hammered against his chest like police pounding on a door just before breaking it down. He didn't dare move but his bow was on the ground to his right with an arrow still nocked to the string. It may as well have been a mile away as the big buck was locked onto him like a fighter pilot locks on to enemy aircraft.

He could feel the buck's eyes scrutinizing him. It wasn't a young and dumb yearling or doe. It was an elder, and big bucks didn't get old by being stupid. It would surely cut and run in a second or two. But it didn't. Instead, it took a hesitant step forward. Troy willed it to take another step; if it did it, would surely go left or right once clear of the thick scrub pines, offering him a broadside shot. If only somehow, he could get his bow in his hands!

The buck suddenly turned its head around, looking back the way it came. Troy quickly and silently grabbed his bow. He almost had it raised when the buck looked forward again. It took two more steps forward and scanned left and right.

A Cooper's hawk screeched overhead just as the deer took a hesitant two more steps, turning to its right. It was now completely broadside to Troy as it lowered its head to graze on some grass.

Troy knew he had to attempt a shot soon. Buck fever was in full force. His body was starting to suffer the effects of a massive adrenaline dump. His vision was tunneled, his hands started to tremble, and his heartbeat was easily over 140.

The buck turned to look back into the jack pines once again as though hearing something behind it. Troy raised his bow, still seated, and smoothly drew the arrow back to full length. Looking through his peep-site he positioned it perfectly, and semi-steadily, on the 30-yard site-pin. He aligned the pin at the buck's side about 6" behind its shoulder. Hoping for a quick double lung kill, he released the arrow. It streaked silently across the distance, but the bow made a soft "twang" despite the attached silencers.

The big buck jumped upwards at the sound just as the arrow impacted its side and blew completely through it. Troy heard the rewarding whack of the arrow impacting flesh and bone. The mortally-wounded deer gave no sign of injury as it fled headlong into the jack pines. Troy could hear it galloping away like a scared horse through the brush.

"Thank you, Jesus!" Troy whispered to himself. His shot may have gone a bit lower than anticipated but it was still a solid hit.

As any deer bow-hunter knows, tracking is an essential art form for the recovery of a wounded deer. Very seldom do they simply drop at the spot they are hit. Troy knew the best thing to do was to wait for at least a half-hour before even attempting to track, as this gives the deer an opportunity to bed down and die. Some mortally wounded deer could cover more than a mile if tracked too quickly.

Troy realized Mitch and Ryan were out scouting their swamp from last night and looking for signs of the mystery animal. He figured Preacher was still sleeping. He decided to have another smoke to calm down—hell, maybe fire up one of his joints and take just a couple hits to smooth out—then make a cursory check of the area to see if there was a decent blood trail. If there was, he would back off and go to the cabin for breakfast and return later with his brothers. If not, maybe he would start a track on his own. Maybe his luck was finally turning, he thought.

It certainly was, but not for the better.

• • • •

CHAPTER 22

Ryan and Mitch headed cautiously back into the swamp with Mitch leading the way. Ryan, his climbing stand strapped to his back, picked his way through the dense swamp. He carried his crossbow cocked with a bolt nocked. This wasn't particularly safe, but he wasn't taking any chances of a surprise attack by anything, human or animal. Mitch carried his compound in his left hand and his pistol in his right.

"This is some thick shit!" Ryan complained in a whisper while slithering over another blowdown. Seconds later he crawled under another one.

"I told you. Unfortunately, it doesn't get any better."

"Did you give any thought to how we'll drag a big buck out of here?"

"Yeah, I did. I figured we'll quarter it like they do big elk and moose in Alaska," answered Mitch.

"Good idea, because dragging one outta here would be a real bitch."

After another 20 minutes of climbing up, over, and under several more blowdowns while dealing with sporadic pockets of mud and water, Mitch stopped and holstered his gun in his waistband. Wiping perspiration from his forehead, he pointed to his ground-blind 25 yards away.

"Sweet spot. I wouldn't have noticed it unless you pointed it out. Where did you see the Dogman at?"

Mitch laughed quietly.

"I saw something over there," he said while gesturing to another deer run that ran at a diagonal behind his blind. "I'm pretty sure it wasn't a Dogman."

"Dude. This is perfect habitat for something like that. I mean, who the hell else would come back here? We could be the first people in here since the Indians," Ryan exclaimed excitedly.

Mitch shook his head and started down the deer run towards where he saw... Whatever he saw the night before. It didn't seem nearly as frightening as the prior evening, now that the sun was up and birds were fluttering by, chirping up a storm. It was cool, about 45 degrees, and a few cumulus clouds floated overhead.

Ryan unslung his tree stand and left it near Mitch's blind as he trudged after him. Mitch slowed ahead and stopped. "It was right around here I first saw it before it ran that way," Mitch said while pointing deeper in the swamp behind them.

Ryan looped around him and started looking for tracks, but the ground was mostly moss- and leaf-covered.

An ear-splitting scream that transformed into a guttural howl erupted suddenly from farther behind them. The horrifying sound echoed all around them long after whatever made it had stopped.

"Jesus, Mary, and Joseph!" Ryan exclaimed as he raised his crossbow in the general direction of the scream. "What the hell was that?"

Mitch drew his pistol and pointed it in the same direction. "That, my brother, is your Dogman."

"Well, screw that. I don't want any part of that shit!" Ryan answered while walking hurriedly back towards Mitch.

"Relax, bro. That sounded about a quarter mile away," Mitch reasoned. The guttural scream repeated but sounded much closer now.

"I've never heard anything like that before. It sounds seriously pissed off, and it's moving towards us, fast! We need to get back to the Suburban," Ryan said, panicked.

Despite it being daylight, the terror of the prior evening was returning. "Calm down, brother. It's not a freaking monster. Think rational, bro. It's probably a bobcat or maybe a cougar," Mitch reasoned, but wasn't so sure himself.

"You said it was almost six feet tall. That sure as hell doesn't fit the description of any bobcat or cougar I'm aware of!" Ryan said.

"Okay. Fair enough. Maybe it's better we hunt elsewhere."

"You think?!"

As Ryan reached to grab his tree stand, he heard sudden movement approaching them from the direction of the last scream. Mitch raised his gun while Ryan dropped his crossbow and drew his pistol as well. Three deer exploded from the underbrush, practically running both the brothers over, zigging and zagging around them before continuing their frantic fleeing from whatever was behind them.

"Holy shit, brother. Those deer are running scared," Ryan said, equally frightened.

"Let's move bro. Go, go, go!" Mitch ordered as they both heard something large coming their way. They started scrambling back towards the Suburban, each stumbling numerous times only to be assisted to their feet by the other. They pushed and pulled each other along while anxiously looking behind them.

They were less than a hundred yards from the Suburban when Mitch fell once again, his boot caught on an unseen vine. As he stumbled face-first to the ground, his gun tumbled from his hand, landing several feet ahead of him. Ryan bent down to assist him as the ungodly scream erupted from only 50 or so yards behind them.

Ryan turned and fired blindly into the thick brush behind them, emptying his 12-round clip. Tiny branches exploded nearby from the lead rounds, shredding pine bark from the trees like a flock of angry woodpeckers. Ryan expertly ejected his magazine, inserted another from his pocket, and stood ready to defend them if anything emerged. His breathing was labored and his heart rate was red-lining.

The swamp was eerily silent now. Ryan heard only the ringing in his ears from the gunshots. Mitch crawled forward and grabbed his gun. Standing, he walked over to Ryan, who was still in a combat-ready stance, and focused towards the threat. Mitch gently placed his hand on his shoulder. Ryan flinched, then relaxed, realizing it was only his brother. "It's okay, bro. I think you scared it away. Did you see it?"

Ryan shook his head, "No, but it was close, and I didn't want it to get any closer, whatever the fuck it was!"

As they walked out of the swamp, both coming down from an adrenaline surge, they were greatly relieved to see the Suburban. The relief was short-lived as Mitch swore. All four tires were flat. On closer inspection, each had a slit in the sidewall.

"It was those fucking rednecks in the stolen car. No doubt about it!" Ryan said.

"Probably. But whatever was chasing us sure as hell wasn't any rednecks," Mitch said, still watching over his shoulder. He sighed heavily, and upon seeing his phone had no service, re-leased a scream almost equal to whatever had been chasing them.

CHAPTER 23

Harley headed home for breakfast. He had arrived at his shop before six. Snake's cousin, Rocco, arrived about a half hour later in his Silverado, pulling a covered utility trailer. Harley helped him load the stolen car parts into the trailer and triple-checked that he knew where he was going when he arrived in Cincinnati. Rocco assured him he knew the place as he had delivered there a year or so ago. Harley reminded him to follow the speed limit. He didn't want to lose $15,000 in stolen auto parts to an overly motivated state trooper.

Harley was bouncing down the main dirt road in his wrecker as it hadn't been plowed smooth in over a month. The log haulers rutted it up worse than usual, he thought as he bounced around inside his cab like a kid on a pogo stick. He slowed the wrecker as he observed two guys ahead standing along the road, waving their arms about.

He buzzed down the window and shifted into neutral, rolling to a stop across the road from them. "Somethin' I can do for ya, boys?"

"As a matter of fact, I hope you can. My brother and I were hunting up the two-track here and some assholes sliced all of my tires. My truck's about a half-mile in. Any chance you can tow me to a tire shop? I got Triple-A," the older and bigger of the two guys said.

"Hell yes, I can. Even better, I have my own shop. I can hook you up with a really fair price on some gently used tires. It's only 15 miles away on the north end of Mio. I don't do

Triple-A, but if you wait for them guys it'll be half a fucking day! I'll only charge ya 60 bucks for the tow."

The guy thought about it for a minute, then said, "Sounds fair to me."

"Good deal. Hop on in. Lucky for you two I was driving my flatbed today. Otherwise, I would have to drive all the way back to the shop and switch rigs. Four flat tires don't do so well on the conventional wreckers."

"I suppose not. Thanks, we appreciate it," the man said while walking around to the passenger side door.

The younger one hopped in first and extended his hand. "I'm Ryan. Pleased to meet you," he said as his brother hopped in and reached across him to shake Harley's hand as well. "I'm Mitch. Thanks again, you're a Godsend."

Harley chuckled. "Shit. I don't know about all that, but I'll get you boys back on the road again without hurting your wallet too bad."

Harley shifted into first and started down the two-track. "Y'all see any deer?"

Harley noticed how the two exchanged glances before the older one finally responded.

"We did, three does practically ran us over. They were running scared shitless from something."

"Probably the Dogman," Harley answered matter-of-factly.

Ryan spoke up excitedly. "I knew it! So there is a Dogman."

Harley laughed before replying, "Sure is, and there's more than one, that's for damn sure."

"Have you seen them?" Ryan asked like an excited kid being told someone saw Santa Claus.

Harley nodded his head and said, "Sure have. I've seen 'em plenty of times. I live just down the road. This thick-ass swamp is the perfect habitat for 'em."

Mitch listened skeptically but said nothing.

"What exactly do they look like?" inquired Ryan.

"Well, they look like a big-ass gnarly wolf, but their face isn't quite right for a wolf. Their snout isn't as long as a wolf, about half so, and their ears are more rounded, almost human-like but not quite. If startled, or wanting to scare ya, they'll stand and walk upright like a bear. They have the Gawd-aw-fullest scream you ever did hear."

"We heard it just this morning. It was chasing the deer, and us, too!" Ryan exclaimed.

"You're lucky. I've seen what's left of deer after they're done with them. They clean 'em like vultures. Nothing left on the bones at all. Looks like them poor deer went into an acid bath or something when they're done."

"So, have you got any of them on film? Like a game camera or something? Seems like if there's so many of them, there would be some captured on film," Mitch said skeptically.

Harley caught his doubtful tone and slammed on the wrecker's brakes. As neither Ryan nor Mitch was belted, they both bounced hard off the dashboard.

"Damn!" Ryan yelled.

"You fucking calling me a liar?" Harley said vehemently while glaring at Mitch.

The brothers were shocked at how the congenial man of just a few seconds ago had completely changed, like Dr. Jekyll and Mr. Hyde.

"Take it easy. I wasn't suggesting that at all. I was just thinking that would be great to have a pic of one of those things.
That's all. I didn't mean any disrespect," Mitch replied with the
most sincerity he could muster, despite meaning exactly what
Harley had thought.

Tension emanated from Harley like heat waves off summer
asphalt. Ryan and Mitch could actually feel it. After a few seconds, Harley shrugged and said, "Apology accepted. Most folks
don't believe they exist, but anyone lives around these parts
knows otherwise. I reckon no one has captured 'em on film
cause they is smarter than any other animal out there. Hell, you
know how smart and weary deer are. Fox too. These things are
ten times smarter. I've tried, I've set game cameras and purposely tried to bait 'em in. I do have a blurry image of one running past but that's it. It's like they knows we're trying to 'film
em.

"Lots of folks have seen them. They're not as widely known
as Bigfoot. Hell, everyone has heard of *them*, but the Michigan
Dogman isn't a Bigfoot. Like I said, it's more dog-like than ape-
like.The first sighting of a Dogman was over a hundred years
ago in Wexford County. Several loggers claimed they saw a sev-
en-foot tall dog-like animal runnin' about their camp. About
50 years later, a man reported being attacked by five wild dogs
with one of them walking on two legs. A couple other sightings were made over the years and usually in the deep forest.
Hell, a bunch of hippies saw one looking inside their camper
one night. They said it had blue eyes and was grinning at 'em.
Rangers and cops have seen 'em too."

"How cool is that!" Ryan exclaimed.

"I suppose there could be some type of undiscovered animal, especially in these thick woods," Mitch conceded.

"That's true. For years, folks up here reported seeing large cat-like creatures in the forest the size of big dogs, but the DNR and other so-called professionals said there weren't any such thing. Shit, my daddy and my brothers, we all knew there were cougars here. We didn't need the fucking DNR to confirm it like they finally did. Give 'em time. They'll confirm the Dogman too."

Harley shifted the wrecker back into first and started back down the two-track. Mitch and Ryan wisely remained silent the remainder of the way to his Suburban.

CHAPTER 24

Damn, Troy thought. The weed Ryan got him was superb. He lie on his back alongside the riverbank, watching the cotton-candy like clouds drift overhead. His nightmare on the plane just yesterday morning seemed like an eternity ago. He was up north in God's country, it was a beautiful morning, and he arrowed a monster buck! Life was good! He could lay here all day, as mellow as he now felt. *Fuck the creditors*, he thought, not to mention the goons that would collect for them. He was in paradise for a week and what a way to start it.

Troy forced himself to get vertical. He checked his cell for the time and was surprised that an hour had elapsed since he shot the buck. He started walking the same way the fox had went along the riverbank earlier, hoping to find a dry way across. He didn't relish getting soaked with cold river water.

He was rewarded after only a few minutes of walking. The river narrowed a bit and an old free-swinging cable bridge with wooden slats was strung across its width about four feet above the water. He hesitantly crossed over. The wooden planks were slippery, as mold covered most of them, but otherwise, the bridge seemed solid. Upon reaching the other side, he walked back to where he had shot the buck.

When he thought he was at the right spot, he started looking closely at the ground and quickly discovered a faint deer run. He was fairly certain it was where the buck had been standing when he first spotted it.

He continued to monitor the ground as well as the sides of the numerous scrub pines, hoping to spot some blood. He was about 20 yards in when he saw red contrasting sharply against the green pine needles. He swiped his finger on the needles and was pleased to see the red was indeed blood. He was even more pleased when he noted it was pinkish color and frothy, indicating a lung hit. Hopefully he had hit both of them. Troy knew a one-lung hit was shit. Healthy deer could go on for miles with one lung, but a double lung usually resulted in a quick death, as well as a quick recovery.

Troy decided to press on with the blood trail, venturing farther into the pines. He left small strips of bright red trail-tape hanging from branches to allow himself to easily find his way back.

His brothers would be upset. Following a blood trail of an arrowed deer, especially one that leads to the recovery of the animal, is a sacred tradition that few people are privileged to participate in. It's as though one is communing with the Native Americans from years earlier, when stalking a wounded deer was not only a specific skill set but a matter of daily sustenance for an entire tribe.

Troy and his brothers understood this. They didn't take hunting lightly and hated the occasion when they could not recover a wounded deer. Hours would be spent searching if needed, perhaps days. Troy lost only one deer he arrowed due to an errant shot. He knew the circle of life went on, and that the dead deer likely fed a bunch of vultures or coyotes, but he had felt sick about not locating it for months afterward.

Troy continued deeper into the scrub pines that were now merging with swampy terrain. He was optimistic as he spotted several other droplets of pinkish blood marking the way like Hansel and Gretel tossing bread-crumbs.

He was walking quietly, following the blood trail, when tall swamp grass in front of him erupted with commotion. The injured buck was bedded down in the grass and now hopped awkwardly away from him.

Troy swore to himself. He could tell by its wobbly gait that it was severely injured, but he now believed he had penetrated only one lung. He was pushing the deer forward when he should have waited longer, allowing it to bed down and die. He decided he would backtrack and return with his brothers later. Hopefully, it would bed down again and die, allowing him to recover it. Those plans were about to change.

The buck was still close enough that he could hear it as it trudged through the thick swamp grass and pockets of water. But he now heard something else running very fast through the same tall grass about sixty feet in front of him. He could see the tall grass tips begin to fold forward, as if under high wind, as whatever it was raced through them unseen.

Another deer? Troy wondered. Whatever it was, it moved fast fast. Seconds later, a low growl and roar radiated from where he last heard the injured buck moving. All hell appeared to be letting loose, as Troy heard thrashing of weeds, growling, and splashing of water. *What the fuck?* thought Troy, as he quickly removed an arrow from his quiver and nocked it to the string with a trembling hand.

Something was attacking his injured trophy buck. He figured it was a cougar, as fast as it had moved, or perhaps a coyote, or even a pack of them. Whatever it was, he wasn't giving up on his buck that easy. He started stalking forward, but cautiously, towards the disturbance only 50 to 60 yards ahead.

When he was within 50 feet of the commotion ahead, it abruptly ceased. He knelt, trying desperately to see through the swamp grass. Troy could now hear tearing and chewing sounds. He finally came to his senses. What was he doing? He only had his bow and arrows and a large hunting knife. How did he expect to fight off a pack of coyotes or a cougar? No buck was worth dying over or being mauled.

He decided to slowly backtrack before he was spotted.

He was only three steps back when his cell phone alarm started clanging. *Holy shit!* He recalled that he had set the alarm when he laid down on the riverbank in case he fell asleep.

The chewing sound stopped as he frantically silenced the alarm.

The swamp grass started slowly bending forward just 50 feet in front of him, as whatever had killed and was eating his buck now crept stealthily towards him. He suddenly remembered that he had a can of bear spray in his fanny pack. He felt better using that than a single shot chance with a bow, especially if he was up against a pack of coyotes. Troy quietly sat his bow on the ground and unzipped his fanny pack. He withdrew the black canister that was roughly the size of a spray paint can. His heart beat in his throat.

"Leave! Go away!" He yelled as he fumbled with the safety release. The grass in front him continued bending forward and he heard a low guttural growl. Troy finally found the safety, pulled the plastic ring off the canister, and directed the nozzle at the grass with his finger on the trigger.

Still kneeling, he recalled one should make themselves as large as possible to ward off predators. He stood on trembling legs while holding the canister with both hands in front of his body. "Fuck off!" He screamed as grass continued to bend towards him, barely ten feet in front of him. He peered intently through the partially-parted grass and thought he saw a figure. It was large and brown. Too big for a cougar or a coyote. But the color was wrong for a bear, as only black bears resided in Michigan. *Wolf?* He thought.

His scream was matched by a scream unlike anything he had ever heard. The brown furry figure now started to rise. Bile raced up his throat as he struggled not to puke.

Troy didn't wait for the figure to clear the tall grass. He depressed the trigger on the can as the unknown animal quickly reached its full height of over six feet tall. Troy's vision was obscured by the fog of pepper spray spewing from the canister, but for just a second Troy thought the animal's face resembled a person's face, but with a small jutting snout covered in fur. Its open mouth revealed long fangs.

That fleeting, partially-obscured glimpse was all he would see of the creature, as during his panicked state, he forgot he was downwind when he sprayed the canister. A large portion of the capsicum blew back on him as well. The concentrated capsicum compound immediately reacted with his eyes, skin, and respiration.

Troy tried desperately to eject the remainder of the can's contents at the creature but had to drop it from his hands to rub his eyes with his palms. His tear ducts immediately emptied, as did his nasal glands and stomach. He backed away blindly from the fiery mist that seemed to be burning his skin, as if someone had soaked him with lighter fluid and set him on fire. He gasped for air as mucus streamed from his nose.

He lost track of the animal that was stalking him just seconds ago, hoping the bear spray had affected it as badly as it was affecting him. For now, the capsicum was the primary threat as he struggled to breathe. Troy collapsed to the ground and took handfuls of mud and smeared them onto his face and in his eyes, hoping for relief from what felt like a thousand hornet stings. If the animal was somehow unaffected, it would surely pounce on him as it had the injured buck, thought Troy. But he was completely and utterly helpless and was now certain he would die in the swamp.

"Brother! I'm here. What's wrong?" He heard Preacher ask. Before he could respond, he felt Preacher's hands on his shoulders.

"Good Lord, is that bear spray?" Preached inquired while coughing and waving his hands around his face to stave off the residual capsicum that was on Troy. "Were you attacked by a bear? Are you hurt?" Preached asked between coughing fits.

Troy tried to speak but his throat was constricted and felt as though he had drunk lava. Preacher quickly pulled a camouflage face mask over his head to offer some protection to his mouth and nose. He again asked if Troy was injured. Troy shook his head.

Preacher, assuming a bear had charged him, wanted to get out of the swamp quickly. He fought back his coughing and helped Troy to his feet, then began guiding him out of the swamp, following the trail tape that Troy had placed earlier. All the while, he looked over his shoulder, but no bear followed.

CHAPTER 25

K arl rode over to Snake's resort in a rage. He was on the Gator as he didn't have any other vehicle available. He covered most of the dozen miles on the ubiquitous ATV trails throughout the forest system.

Snake was behind the rental cabins chopping wood with a five-pound ax. Snake looked every bit of the tough ex-con, half Native-American that he was. He was tall, dark-skinned, and heavily muscled, with tattoos covering almost all of his exposed skin. Several black teardrop tats were scattered under his right eye—one for each man he killed. His long black hair was knotted into a ponytail that extended to the middle of his back.

Upon seeing Karl drive up, Snake buried the ax-head into the stump he was splitting pine logs on and smiled. "You look seriously pissed off. Did that fine looking piece of ass leave you?" He teased.

Karl sighed. He sure as hell didn't want to talk about it. He wanted to forget about it. He just grimaced and shook his head slightly.

"No worries," Snake said. "Talk when you want to talk about it. What can I get you?"

"I need something strong, but not too strong that I can't function. Harley wants me to chop up a couple of cars in the next couple of days. I want to be numb when I'm doing it. Oh, and I need some of the usual shit."

Snake grinned and remarked, "So she hasn't left you yet, but you just don't want to think about her for a while. Let me guess, she had a go at Harley, and you walked in on 'em. I always knew you two wouldn't last."

Karl wasn't in the mood, and he badly needed to release some of his pent-up stress. Snake was absolutely the wrong guy to mess with, but right now Karl didn't really give a shit. "Fuck you!" He yelled, then charged him.

Snake was shocked. Karl had never been aggressive towards him, not even playfully in the ten years he knew him. Most folks were scared shitless of Snake, and for good reason. Snake had watched Karl beat down a few loudmouth tourists over the years, but that was about it.

The element of complete surprise was the only reason Karl got to him untouched; otherwise, Snake would have knocked him out as soon as he entered his reach. Instead, Karl tackled Snake to the ground. Snake cracked his head, hard, on one of the pine logs he hadn't split yet. He grunted in pain while blinking back his receding vision. *Shit,* he thought in disbelief. Karl had almost rendered him unconscious.

Three barely-teens who were staying with their parents in a couple of rental cabins upfront happened upon them. They stayed back and watched the melee. This was the most excitement they had experienced since arriving two days ago. Each of them raised their cell phones to record the fight.

Karl scrambled up Snake's huge frame and sat on his stomach while raining down rabbit punches towards his face. Snake, still a bit dazed, started to slap the blows away like he would mosquitoes. "Fuck's wrong with you, Karl?! Knock this shit off 'fore I kill your sorry ass!"

"Go for it, bitch!" Karl yelled back, continuing with his punches. One slipped through and split Snake's lip.

Snake's eyes narrowed and his eyebrows furrowed tight together. He grabbed Karl's upper arms with both of his hands in a powerful grip and pulled him forward. As Karl's upper body and face came closer to his, Snake sprang his head forward, smashing his forehead into Karl's nose.

Karl howled in pain as blood flowed freely from his shattered nose, staining Snake's white tank top red. Snake shot his right arm behind Karl's head and grabbed his right wrist with his left hand, securing Karl tightly in a front headlock. He now squeezed his powerful arms tightly around Karl's neck and rolled over. During the roll, Karl raised his right knee hard into Snake's groin. His grip weakened from the blow, allowing Karl to slither out from underneath him like a lizard.

Karl was attempting to stand when Snake grabbed his boot and started hauling him back towards him, where he was still prone on the ground. Karl kicked at him with his other hand and managed to stand. Snake scrambled to his feet as well. Both men were hunched forward like wrestlers looking for a takedown. Each of them was breathing heavily. The kids nearby were enjoying the fight immensely, wondering how many likes they would generate on Instagram.

Snake licked the blood from his split lip, then spit, "You have enough? If not, I'm gonna seriously fuck you up, and I really don't want to do that."

Karl's nose was still leaking blood and he was breathing laboriously, but deep inside, he felt great. He hadn't felt such a visceral feeling like this in a long time. It wasn't better than sex, but it was close, he thought. "What makes you think you can? I'm not some prison bitch. Let's finish this fucker!"

Karl charged him once again. This time Snake anticipated it, easily ducking the telegraphed wild right-hook that Karl led with. While still crouched low, Snake unleashed his own right hook, twisting his waist to obtain maximum power. His punch landed squarely in Karl's stomach and literally lifted him off his feet several inches. Karl doubled over, gasping for air. Snake now delivered a punishing elbow strike to the base of Karl's neck. The force of the blow propelled Karl face-first into the dirt and rendered him unconscious.

The kids applauded wildly and cheered the victor. Snake, aware of them for the first time, bowed slightly, then shooed them away. He dusted himself off and walked towards his cabin to fill Karl's order.

CHAPTER 26

Mitch and Ryan were almost back to the cabin. Mitch's Suburban had slightly used tires but at least they were holding air.

"That Harley guy seems like a decent sort. We were fortunate he was driving by at the time he was," Ryan commented.

"He saved our ass for sure," Mitch replied. "Triple-A would have taken a lot longer. He was nice enough, but man, he sure got pissed off when he thought I doubted his stories about the Dogman."

"I'm kind of surprised you're still a doubter myself. I mean, jeesh, we were chased by one."

"We were chased by something, brother, but I don't know what."

"Mom should have named you Thomas," Ryan replied.

Mitch looked at him with a puzzled expression.

"As in Doubting Thomas. When's the last time you been to mass, bro?" Ryan chided.

Mitch sighed. "It's been a while, but don't tell Mom or Preacher."

"Well, get back to it, bro. I'm hoping to need a godfather someday soon."

"You have a godfather."

"Damn, for a cop, you sure are slow. I'm talking about for my future child."

"Is Frankie pregnant?" Mitch asked with excitement.

"We're not sure yet, but she's several weeks late and a pharmacy prego test says she is, but keep a lid on it. I don't want to tell everyone yet. You're the first to know."

"And if she is, you guys are going to ask me to be the godfather? What about Preacher?"

"Preacher would be a great choice, too, but it'll be you."

Mitch smiled widely and said, "I would be honored. Congrats brother."

"Thanks, but I don't want to jinx it so let's drop it for now."

• • • •

IT WAS ALMOST ONE O'CLOCK as they arrived at the cabin. Preacher and Troy were walking towards them. Mitch could see that Preacher was helping Troy walk.

"Uh-oh! That doesn't look good," Ryan commented. They both jumped out of the Suburban and jogged towards their brothers.

Once Mitch heard Troy was exposed to concentrated capsicum, he wisely didn't let him flush his face with water. Mitch knew from the pepper spray he carried as a police officer that fresh air was the best thing to clear it up. Water alone would not do the trick; in fact, it would make it worse, as pepper spray was oil-based.

Mitch led Troy to the shower and had him lather his face up with shampoo without water. He then wiped the shampoo off with a washcloth. He made Troy repeat the process three times. The last time he instructed Troy to rinse off his exposed face and hands with a liberal amount of cold water, then scrub his face dry with a towel.

Troy finally started to get some relief from the constant burning. Mitch led him to the kitchen table and told him to lay his head back while he turned the ceiling fan on high. Preacher brought him two Advil for the pain and Troy greedily swallowed them down.

"Are you certain we shouldn't take him to a hospital?" Preacher asked Mitch with concern.

"I don't need a hospital," Troy said. "I'm feeling a lot better already. Thanks, guys. I thought I was going to die out there." Preacher had already filled them in on what little he knew had happened, but Troy hadn't been able to talk very well until now. "Ryan's right. There is a fucking monster out there! I saw it. It was huge and had a furry human-looking face. I swear it was going to kill me. I shot a huge buck and was following the blood trail when this thing came from out of nowhere. It attacked my wounded buck and then started eating it!"

"It came after us too!" Ryan said excitedly. "It chased us all the way back to the Suburban. I emptied my clip at the damn thing just to stop it."

"Did you hit it?" Troy asked.

"I don't know. I don't think so. I was more or less just shooting in the direction I heard it coming from. Maybe?" Ryan said with a shrug.

Preacher looked back and forth between Ryan and Troy in astonishment. "Did you see it, Mitch?" He asked.

Mitch sighed heavily. "I don't know what I saw, but Ryan is correct. Whatever it was, it was chasing us.

"Dammit, Mitch, do you need the thing to stand right in front of you before you believe in it? You know that wasn't a bear or anything else normal. Its growl alone is unlike anything we've ever heard," Ryan exclaimed in frustration.

Mitch walked over to the fridge and grabbed a couple of handfuls of beer bottles from within, passing them around. The brothers each drank their first few swigs in silence. All of them were processing the unbelievable morning they had.

Ryan broke the silence. "You shot a buck?" He said to Troy.

"Damn straight. It was a huge 12-pointer. I shot across the river and nailed it. I was going to wait for you guys but wasn't sure when you would be back, so I started a preliminary track and jumped it almost immediately."

"You could have come and got me," Preacher said.

"I know. I should have but I got excited and just wanted to get after it."

"You saw this thing, whatever it was, eating your buck?" Mitch inquired.

"Well, I didn't exactly see it eating the buck, but I could hear it," Troy answered.

"Just curious, you didn't smoke any weed before your hunt, did ya?"

"Dammit, brother. You and Ryan also saw it. Why are you such a dick all the time?"

"We didn't see very much but something was definitely chasing us. I'm not trying to be a dick, bro. I'm just gathering facts."

"Why don't you stop being a cop for one damn minute. You want facts. This is a fact. Something fucking strange is out in that swamp. You encountered it, Ryan encountered it, and I did, too!"

"I notice you didn't answer my question about smoking dope."

"Seriously, brother! Fuck the dope. That had nothing to do with it."

"How about we all relax," Preacher interjected. "I'm sure everyone is hungry. I've been a bit busy this morning, but I brought up a venison sausage roll stuffed with jalapeño and cheddar cheese. I'll slice that up and use some of the Amish bread the cabin owner left us for sandwiches. Margie sent up some of her world-famous potato salad as well."

"That sounds great, Preacher. I've been thinking about her potato salad since the last camp." Troy replied.

Ryan and Mitch grunted their approval.

Several minutes, and two beers each, later, the brothers gathered outside on the porch drinking beer, eating venison sandwiches and red-skin potato salad. The cool morning was replaced with a mild afternoon temperature in the mid-60s. A nearby woodpecker pounded away on a tree.

"Are you going to report your tires being slashed?" Preacher asked Mitch.

"I already called it in when we were in Mio. The dispatcher said they were short-staffed and very busy. Once I told her I was an officer she transferred me to a supervisor with the Michigan State Police. He agreed to take the report over the phone."

"Now that's the *real* police," Ryan teased, knowing the good-natured rivalry between the state police and city police officers.

Mitch flipped him the bird.

Preacher asked, "Are they going to question those two rednecks that almost hit your Suburban yesterday?"

"I mentioned the incident to him and described where they lived. He said he would have someone question them when they got a chance. It's not like they're going to fess up to it."

"I suppose, but still, it'll at least make them think twice about doing something stupid again," Preacher reasoned.

"Yeah, maybe."

"We need to report this crazy animal thing to the DNR or the forest rangers," Troy said.

"I agree. Whatever it is, it's dangerous, and rifle season is coming up in a few weeks. I would hate for someone to get killed by it," Ryan added.

Mitch asked, "And what exactly should we tell them? A creature chased us. We have no photos, no prints, nada, zero, zilch to prove anything. We'll be like those bozos that report UFOs. It's probably a rabid bear."

Ryan vigorously shook his head, as did Troy. "It wasn't a bear!" Ryan challenged Mitch.

"I don't know that it wasn't. It sure seems a lot more likely than some kind of unknown creature like 'Bigfoot.'" Mitch said, using air quotes.

"Even if it is a bear, I think the DNR needs to know something vicious is in the area," Preacher reasoned.

"Go ahead, notify them, but you'll have to drive halfway to town to get cell service," Mitch replied. "Why don't we wait until the end of the week? Maybe we'll have a pic of it on a trail cam by then."

"Whatever," Troy replied.

"I just realized I left my climbing stand at your ground blind," Ryan said to Mitch, who was rocking steadily in an old wooden rocking chair.

"Why don't you go get it? I'll wait here for you." Mitch replied with a slight grin.

Ryan flipped him off and smiled as well.

"My fucking bow is still in the swamp," Troy said, "and it can stay there. I'll use Ryan's spare one if that's okay. But I'm not hunting anywhere near that swamp."

"As long as you don't hunt near my spot." Preacher replied. "I set up my tree stand about a hundred yards that way. There's a nice well-traveled run and someone placed a salt lick out."

Mitch laughed. "Are you ever going to venture farther than a hundred yards from a cabin, Preacher?"

It was an old joke. Preacher never went too far from the cabin. He would never admit it, but the other brothers suspected he was a bit scared to be in the woods alone. "Why should I when I get a deer nearly every other year?" Preacher said.

"I suppose if you're happy with a doe, it's okay." Ryan chimed in.

"You young-uns will learn someday that does and bucks both taste the same," Preacher countered.

"Not true, Preacher. Those small yearlings you get are much more tender." Troy added as Mitch and Ryan joined him in laughter.

"Keep it up and you'll be fixing your own meals the remainder of the week," Preacher warned while stabbing his finger at them.

"What time are we leaving for wings and women?" asked Troy, who was now feeling much better.

"Wings and beer, not women," Preacher admonished.

"Soon as we all get back from the evening hunt, I suppose," answered Mitch.

"Sounds like a plan," Ryan quipped.

"Looks like a storm might be rolling in." Preacher gestured to the eastern sky, where, off in the distance, a group of black clouds was forming.

"Huh," Ryan said. "There's only a 10 percent chance of that, according to my weather app earlier when we were in town."

"The percentages don't always work out for you, even when they are stacked in your favor," Troy said with conviction from experience at the poker tables. No one at the time realized how prophetic that observation would be.

CHAPTER 27

J esse kept the Shelby on the back roads, but was able to open it up on a couple of stretches long enough to get Sue Ellen really excited. So much so, in fact, that she leaned over and whispered into his ear, over the car's roaring engine, in explicit detail what she wanted to do to him. He wasn't sure if it was the car ride or her participation in puncturing the tires on the Suburban in the woods earlier that had her so excited.

Jesse couldn't believe his luck at spotting the same assholes again turning down the two-track. He drove past, figuring they were going hunting, but returned several minutes later. He and Sue Ellen walked up the two-track until they found the truck. When he unsheathed his buck-knife, she asked if she could help him slice the tires. She giggled like a schoolgirl as they ran down the two-track afterward back to the Shelby.

It didn't matter what the case of her excitement was: he wasn't about to miss a chance at what she promised to do to him. He downshifted the Shelby and turned right onto a little-used road and drove it back to a scenic lookout over the Au Sable River. Fortunately, it was deserted. Sue Ellen led him down to the riverbank and eagerly began stripping off his clothes. Jesse retained his cell phone and filmed the time she spent below his waist. He planned on saving it and sending it to Karl the next time he pissed him off.

• • • •

KARL RODE THE ATV BACK to their home a lot slower than he did on the trip to Snake's place. He was careful not to hit too many bumps, as he had a terrific headache and his nose was pulsating with each heart-beat. Snake had fixed him up with some good shit he called "the trifecta." Karl was already feeling better from the mixture of Adderall, Oxycodone, and just a touch of cocaine thrown in. It was painful to snort through a broken nose, but the aftereffects were worth it.

Karl was going to make Sue Ellen beg for it. He couldn't believe she disrespected him like that. She relied on him for her daily fix of shit. Well, no more free fucking lunch. She was going to have to earn it from now on. He was still furious at Jesse but didn't feel the need to kill him as soon as he saw him. Someone once said revenge was a dish best served cold. He would serve Jesse up later. The fight with Snake and the drugs had helped smooth out his rage. He would set his anger aside for now as he and Jesse needed to chop the cars before Harley got home tonight, or he would be pissed. Harley pissed off was not a pretty sight.

The last time Karl and Harley seriously argued was over a year ago. Harley didn't take his aggression out on Karl but rather transferred it to a couple of unfortunate fly fishermen from a downriver Detroit community who happened to be in the wrong place at the wrong time. The pair of missing fishermen was recently featured on a national TV investigative show as it had been a year since their disappearance. Their whereabouts were still unknown to everybody but Karl, Harley, and Jesse.

Karl recalled how he and Harley had trekked through the woods early one morning last year for almost a half-hour to his favorite fishing hole for brown trout. While walking there, Harley started on him about having Sue Ellen living at the house. Karl assured him she was not going to be a problem, but the argument got heated. Karl wisely backed off. The brothers had just emerged to their secret spot when they discovered two men putting on waders and getting ready to fish the hole. A canoe rested on the riverbank near them.

It may have not been a problem until one of the guys looked at them and said, "Sorry, boys, we got here first." Harley went off on a rant about how he was born and raised here and that they were just tourists. Before Karl could say or do anything, Harley went after the guys. Both of them were beefy and much younger than Harley. It didn't matter. Fueled by the recent argument, Harley brutally beat both of them, warning Karl to stay out of it.

After only a minute or so, both of the fishermen were on the ground, trying to crawl away from the madman. Karl urged Harley to let them go but he just glared at Karl, then picked up a nearby dead tree limb that was a bit bigger than a baseball bat. He repeatedly battered it over one of their heads until the man collapsed and the tree limb snapped in half. The ground beneath the fisherman's head was splattered with blood.

The other guy scrambled to his feet and pulled a long fish fillet knife from his belt, holding it in front of him while screaming and crying for Harley to leave. The guy could see his buddy was dead as his head was half caved in. Harley pulled his 45 from his waistband and shot him twice, once in the chest and once in the face.

Karl, in a near panic, finally convinced Harley they had better get out of there. They ran back to their truck. They returned hours later with Jesse and discovered the bodies were still there. Fortunately, feral animals had not discovered them yet.

They wrapped the cadavers up in blue vinyl tarps and dragged them through the woods to the truck. They returned for the fishermen's canoe and other gear, making sure nothing was left behind.

Later that evening the bodies were butchered and fed to the hogs. The remaining bits of bone were raked up and later tossed into the Au Sable. The canoe was cut up with a Sawzall and buried in a remote part of the forest several miles from their property. The remaining personal effects—clothes, tackle, life-vests—were burned in a huge bonfire.

Karl shook his head to help erase the memory like an Etch A Sketch. By the time he was almost home, he was feeling much better, physically and mentally. The drug trifecta was working its magic.

He glimpsed blue through the pine trees as he approached the driveway. A car was stopped at the gate. Karl's heart rate started to accelerate wildly. It was a Michigan State Police car.

Oh, shit on me, Karl thought. He was violating several laws. He was operating an ATV on the roadway. He was not wearing a helmet. He was high and in possession of drugs. To make matters even worse, he had two outstanding misdemeanor warrants for disorderly conduct out of Grayling. He didn't know what the trooper wanted but suspected he was following up on the missing Census worker from yesterday.

Harley had wisely told Karl to remove the GPS from the dead guy's pickup. Harley later drove it to several other locations before finally tossing it into the Au Sable River 15 miles from their home. In all likelihood, the trooper was on routine follow-up at all stops the man was known to have made, but Karl wasn't about to stop and ask.

An impossibly large bald trooper, in an impeccable blue MSP uniform that strained to contain his muscular frame, was standing at the locked gate, reading the numerous signs warning of death if someone was foolish enough to trespass. Karl decided to cruise past as though it wasn't his home. The trooper turned and made eye contact with him before he could turn away. The trooper made a come here gesture with his hand. Karl did the only thing he could: he accelerated the Gator to full speed. It fishtailed wildly and showered stones and dirt in the air behind it like a rooster-tail from a ski-boat.

The trooper jumped into his cruiser, slammed it into reverse, and rapidly did a reverse J-turn out of the driveway. He then dropped the gear selector into drive and pounded the accelerator, while flipping on his overhead lights and activating the siren. He didn't bother to call it in, as he knew he didn't stand a chance of catching the ATV as it could simply turn into the woods at any second. He wouldn't possibly be able to give chase when it did, but that didn't mean he was about to let a guy just cruise by him while flaunting the law.

Karl glanced back and saw the unique single red bubble design on the MSP car activate. He cursed and raced straight ahead, knowing that a tight hiking trail was just a quarter-mile ahead—one he could navigate but the police car couldn't. A curve was coming up and Karl cringed as he saw the Shelby come around it, straight towards Karl and the rapidly closing Michigan State police car.

CHAPTER 28

L ike a war veteran able to hear an approaching helicopter before anyone else could, Mitch heard the police siren before his brothers. "MSP car approaching," He said between sips of his beer. The brothers were target shooting with their bows at an archery foam block set up 25 yards away.

"Hope you don't have any outstanding warrants, bro," Mitch quipped.

"Naw, I'm good. At least none that anyone will extradite me for," he replied.

No one was certain if he was joking or not. Just then, the others could hear the siren.

"How do you do that?" Ryan asked incredulously.

"It's my element, bro," Mitch responded.

"But it could be an ambulance or a firetruck," Preacher offered.

"Nah. It's the state police. Their siren has a unique pitch and sound," Mitch replied.

They could now also hear the throaty roar of the Shelby as it approached their driveway and flew past at over 85 mph, which was way too fast for a dirt and gravel road in poor shape to begin with. The police car roared by seconds later.

"It's a pursuit, and it sure sounds like that Shelby from yesterday," Mitch offered.

"It sure does. I hope they catch those redneck bastards," Ryan said.

"My money is on the Shelby," Troy offered.

"I just pray no one gets hurt. Those chases are too dangerous," Preacher chipped in from his rocking chair.

"So, we should just let every criminal that flees get away?" Mitch asked.

Preacher took another pull on his beer, then said, "Relax, officer. I'm just making a statement and offering a prayer for all involved."

"Yeah. Well, if it's the same assholes that sliced my tires, I hope they wrap that Shelby around a tree and get ejected," Mitch replied angrily, and stormed into the cabin.

Ryan shot Preacher an admonishing look. Preacher shrugged his shoulders and took another sip of beer.

"He's kind of sensitive when it comes to his brothers in blue. He thinks despite what we see on the news that they can do no wrong," Troy remarked.

Ryan glared at Troy and half-whispered, "That's enough. We came here to have a good time, not to fight amongst ourselves."

"Yeah, well, how's that working out so far?" Troy said as he let loose with an arrow that perfectly impacted the center circle of the target.

Mitch grabbed his fourth beer of the afternoon and stretched out on the overstuffed sofa next to the fieldstone fireplace. Last night's fire was long gone, but a few remnants of partially burnt pine logs still smoldered. Thin tendrils of smoke drifted lazily upward into the chimney. The agreeable aroma of woodsmoke combined with last evening's cigars relaxed him a tad.

Mitch sighed and took a pull from his beer. Thus far the annual hunting trip was anything but dull, but it sure as hell wasn't relaxing. If this kept up, he would need another vacation after this to unwind.

He felt the familiar pull begin and thought, *Not now, please not now!* It was just a gentle resistance at first, like the feeling he got when canoeing against the current, but he knew it would intensify. It always did. Sometimes it progressed quickly. The gentle pushback of the current could soon transition into a continuous series of waves, each bigger than the last, until he was eventually capsized, and struggling not to drown in the depths of depression. Sometimes, it came in slowly like the tide. Its progress, although steady, offered him more time to adapt.

He thought back to his freshman year of high school when the darkness first emerged. He was always the fun-loving adventurous kid that others easily flocked to. A smile was always plastered on his face. His perpetual happiness seemed infectious to those around him. His parents noticed it first. He started spending more time alone and wasn't smiling nearly as much. Sometimes on a weekend, he wouldn't emerge from his bedroom the entire day except to eat. When they asked, he simply told them he was tired or catching up on his reading.

They didn't think too much of it as the following weekend his smile would return, and he was back to normal. He self-diagnosed himself one evening in his sophomore year of high school after reading a book about depression. When he finished the chapter regarding bipolar disorder, he was relieved to realize so many others suffered from it. Most of them suffered in silence, as he did. People were not as open and understanding of mental illnesses then as they were now, Mitch thought.

He didn't tell any of his friends, not even his brothers, until years later. He reluctantly shared the self-diagnosis with his

parents during his junior year of high school. They were skeptical at first, but he finally confided how bad it was. He informed
them that he was having recurring thoughts of suicide. His parents immediately arranged for him to see a therapist.

The bi-monthly visits to the therapist helped him navigate
the early years of his disease. He had managed it for the past
30 odd years, but even though his lows were less frequent now,
when they came, they packed a serious punch.

Mitch realized that by tomorrow evening at the latest, he
would be struggling to function, even with his meds, and only
time would tell how long the episode would last. The thought
that his entire remaining time at deer camp could be jeopar-
dized by a low episode was too much to handle combined with
everything else that already occurred. He cursed and hurled his
now empty beer bottle into the fireplace, then jumped up and
flipped over the nearby coffee table before storming out the
back door just as Preacher ran in the front.

CHAPTER 29

D*amn, this cop can drive!* Jesse thought as he saw the police car closing on him. Jesse needed to get to asphalt roads, and soon, as the Shelby wasn't designed to handle well on a mostly dirt road. He nearly lost it on the last curve, barely staying out of a ditch. Sue Ellen was shouting encouragement at him. She was really enjoying it. Jesse was scared shitless. He had never been to actual jail. He did a few weeks in juvey but that was different. He sure as hell didn't want to be locked up.

Jesse forced himself to think through the problem. That is what Harley always told him: think it through. Jesse knew that the cop had surely called in the pursuit and his buddies were coming, but he also knew that it could likely still be several minutes before any arrived. His window of opportunity was rapidly closing, but still open.

Jesse also knew that most of the state police were not from the area as they rotated them around a lot. Jesse was born and raised here so he knew every shortcut there was. That was his best chance, using his superior knowledge of the area to his advantage. Karl couldn't help him as the Gator simply couldn't keep up with their speeds. *Not that Karl would be in a helping mood anyhow.*

Jesse finally reached an asphalt road and raced through the Shelby's gears like a pro. He gained some quick ground on the cop car. He power-slid through a tight curve then continued to fry the pavement. Jesse realized he was coming up to a seasonal dirt road that he knew was completely washed out near the bottom of a ravine from recent heavy rains. Jesse was just there yesterday checking his traps. If he hadn't been on the ATV, he would never have made it through.

Jesse turned onto it and slowed to allow the trooper to regain his lost ground. He smiled as he saw the police car quickly catching up. When the police car was almost at his bumper, Jesse floored the Shelby once again. After less than a quarter-mile, the road started to descend steeply. He told Sue Ellen to hang on as he suddenly downshifted and braked hard while steering as far to the right as he could without going into the pines. Pine branches slapped against the passenger side of the car like giant rollers in a drive-thru car wash.

As he hoped, the pursuing trooper braked a bit late, and not as hard. The patrol car sailed past him into the soft sand that had pooled across the bottom of the ravine. It slid twenty yards into the soft sand, all of its wheels buried to the frame. Sand flew up into the air and the car was completely lost in a temporary cloud.

"Hell yes!" Jesse yelled happily as he stopped the Shelby just before reaching the soft sand. Sue Ellen leaned over and kissed him hard on the lips, apparently in appreciation of not getting them arrested. As the sand settled ahead, Jesse saw the trooper roll out his door and draw his handgun. Was the crazy bastard going to shoot him? Jesse wondered. *Do they do that for a stolen car?* He wasn't about to stick around to find out.

Jesse pulled away from Sue Ellen's embrace and quickly shifted the Shelby into reverse. He accelerated too rapidly, causing the rear tires to spin wildly. He eased off the accelerator a tad until they finally regained traction. He continued to reverse the few hundred feet back to the main road. Fortunately, the trooper didn't shoot.

As Jesse raced back towards his home, he prayed back-up officers were not yet in the area.

Sue Ellen smiled wickedly at him, realizing she was falling for the kid. He was reckless, wild, and fun, Karl was starting to bore her. Maybe it was time for her to leave him, or even better, for him to leave them. She had some very dark thoughts on the way back to their place. She wasn't bothered by the fact that they excited her.

• • • •

CHAPTER 30

Harley wasn't happy. After getting the tourists back on the road with some gently used tires, he headed back home for a late lunch, but nobody was home. To make matters worse, the Shelby was gone, and Jesse's truck was not parted out yet.

Harley was in the barn sipping on his third beer, getting madder by the bottle, when he heard the Gator approaching. A minute later, Karl walked in, looking worse than usual.

"What the hell happened to you now?" Harley asked upon seeing Karl's bloodied shirt and cotton protruding from his nostrils.

"No big deal. Snake and I had a slight disagreement," Karl said with a dismissive gesture, like he was swatting at a fly.

Harley's eyebrows arched as he asked with a doubtful tone, "You got into it with Snake?"

"Like I said, it was no big deal."

"You get into a fight with Snake and don't end up dead or in the emergency room, it's a big fucking deal," Harley countered. He then threw his hands up in the air and said, "Whatever, but why the hell is your truck still in one piece, and where's Jesse?"

Karl sighed and looked down before saying, "Last I saw him, the State boys were chasing him in the Shelby."

Harley blew a gasket. He yelled and screamed unintelligible words and combined swear words in a fashion Karl had never heard, before finally stopping to catch his breath. He simply stared at Karl for a long time without saying anything, like a judge scrutinizing an unbelievable witness on the stand.

"I can't control the dickhead anymore. He's a grown-ass man now. He took off in the Shelby a few hours ago with Sue Ellen. I was in the cabin. I had no idea he was going to do such a stupid stunt like that," Karl offered feebly in his own defense.

The Shelby's powerful engine could be heard approaching the barn. Karl peeked out of a slit in the mostly boarded-up window. "It looks like he lost them."

Harley pressed the button for the automatic overhead door. The metal door jangled and creaked slowly upwards. Sunlight spilled inside just before the Shelby did. Harley hit the button again to close the door as Sue Ellen and Jesse climbed out.

Jesse nodded at Harley and ignored Karl.

Harley hurled his now empty beer bottle at Jesse's head. Jesse reflexively lifted his left forearm to protect his face. It shattered against his arm. "Shit!" Jesse yelped in both pain and surprise. Harley shot forward the second he launched the bottle, covering the 15 feet between them in a flash. Upon reaching Jesse he roughly shoved him with both hands in the chest. Harley's momentum, combined with the force of the shove, propelled Jesse backward off his feet. He landed hard on the Shelby's hood.

Just as Jesse was starting to roll off, Harley grabbed his boot and walked backward. Jesse was pulled off the hood. The back of his head slammed against the front bumper on the way down, just before his ass impacted the cement oiled-stained floor.

Sue Ellen screamed for Harley to stop. Karl watched the action with a grin and some serious feelings of satisfaction. As Jesse was struggling to get up, Harley dragged him across the floor to a nearby chain that was suspended to a steel girder and a heavy-duty pulley that they used for lifting engines from vehicles. Harley wrapped the chain around Jesse's feet and locked it in place with a large padlock, then walked back to the other side of the garage and hit the remote.

Sue Ellen watched helplessly as Jesse was lifted slowly off the ground upside down. Harley stopped the motor when Jesse's head was about six feet from the floor. Karl grabbed a Sawzall from the bench and fired it up, then started towards Jesse. Sue Ellen screamed in horror and ran between them. Karl gulped as he realized that the shit was about to get real.

CHAPTER 31

It was nearly 4 o'clock. Mitch had been gone for over two hours. Troy was suited up in his Realtree camo and carried Ryan's compound. "You ready to roll?" He asked Ryan, who was camo upped as well but standing in the living room looking uncertain about leaving.

"Go, go, he'll be fine. It's obvious he's having one of his episodes. He'll be fine. He always is, but please take a few minutes while out there to pray this episode is a short one, so his whole week isn't ruined," Preacher said.

"And ours, too," Troy added. "What?" He said when both of them looked at him reproachfully. "It's true. When he's down, we're all brought down. I didn't travel over a thousand miles to be depressed. If he wants to be, well...Whatever."

"Seriously, Troy? You actually think he wants to be depressed? It's a disease. He can't control it," Preacher explained.

"Well, maybe, but we all got our own problems, is all I'm saying."

Ryan looked at Troy and shook his head. "You are unbelievable sometimes. Let's go. I need some time alone in the woods."

"Be careful, guys, and good luck," Preacher said as they left. He watched them load up in Ryan's truck and head down the driveway.

Preacher walked into his bedroom and closed the door. Sitting on the edge of the bed, he closed his eyes, made the sign of the cross, and prayed for all his brothers. He spoke briefly with his deceased father, asking him to watch over them and unite them as well.

Finished with his prayers, Preacher now suited up for his hunt. He left Mitch a note on the table advising him that he was in his tree stand not too far in front of the cabin. He asked that Mitch ring the rusted dinner bell that was attached to the front porch when he returned so he knew he was safe.

As Preacher headed out the door, he could feel the temperature dropping and observed that the sky had darkened considerably. Rain was coming soon. Hopefully not until dusk, as he wasn't wearing his Gortex rain gear, nor did he want to go change into it. Their father always said that an approaching storm was the best time to hunt as it got the deer moving.

Preacher was barely 20 yards from the cabin when a doe bounded across the trail and a small basket-racked six-point buck charged after it. Both disappeared into the bushy pines with barely a sound.

Preacher hurried his pace to get to his tree stand. *Some fresh venison tenderloins would cheer all of us up*, he thought.

After settling down in the ladder stand that was situated 15 feet off the ground, Preacher focused on his surroundings. Twenty yards in front of him was a heavily-traveled deer run that went from east to west thru the jack pines. His stand was on the edge of a small clearing amid the squatty jack pines, most barely six feet tall. They resembled Christmas trees. Preacher knew that they were also the nesting site of a nearly extinct species of bird, the Kirtland's warbler. The small warbler loved to nest in the pines.

Preacher didn't see any warblers, only a few blue jays and a black squirrel. Preacher's stand was secured to one of the odd tall oaks that were interspersed amongst the pines. It still held most of its leaves, but they were starting to fall, as were the acorns that the deer loved to feed on. If Preacher craned his neck to his left, he could see the roof of the cabin about a hundred yards away.

Odd, he thought. It was covered with hundreds of crows. For some reason, his mood suddenly darkened, mirroring the approaching storm clouds. He shivered involuntarily, though not from the rapidly cooling temperature, and felt an intense bout of despair and torment unlike ever before.

Despair wasn't exactly it, he thought, trying to grapple with the unease taking over his mind and body. He couldn't recall ever having a feeling this dark and intense in his lifetime. Was he having a panic attack? Some kind of breakdown?

Unexpectedly, he now had complete clarity on what he was feeling. Foreboding! He was certain, as he was that it was going to rain any minute, that something terrible was going to occur soon.

The dinner bell now rang at the cabin. The crows launched from the roof in unison like a dark plague and flew towards his tree. As they passed over, Preacher heard the beating of their wings and their incessant cries. He had a sudden bout of nausea that caused him to unexpectedly vomit from the stand. When he raised his head, the crows were gone, and it began to rain, huge cold drops that were soon accompanied by his tears. Why was he crying? He hadn't cried since his father's funeral many years ago.

He lowered his head again and muttered a quick prayer, asking God to deliver him from the overwhelming feeling of pure evil and misery he was inexplicably feeling. No sooner had he completed his prayer than a wide bolt of lightning zig-zagged down from the darkest cloud above and struck something nearby. Preacher involuntarily yelped in fear as he was blinded by the brief brilliant flash, while the thunder rumbled immediately overhead like a marching band's drum section doing a frenetic solo.

Dear God, what's happening to me? He thought again, as he scrambled down the ladder of the stand and jogged through the pines towards the cabin. He was now certain, beyond any doubt, that he had to convince his brothers to end their hunting trip and return home immediately—or something horrific was going to happen to them.

CHAPTER 32

"Move out of the way, woman, or I'll saw you in half!" Harley yelled over the shrill sound of the Sawzall blade ratcheting back and forth. Sue Ellen stood her ground, biting her lower lip as she raised her hands in front of her. There was something about Harley's eyes. They were menacing, like shark eyes, unblinking and projecting pure evil.

Karl saw this look before; he knew Harley's threat was serious. At the same time, he felt betrayed that Sue Ellen had run off with Jesse, but he sure didn't want her killed, or Jesse either. *Well, maybe Jesse, but certainly not Sue Ellen*, he thought.

"Good Lord, Harley, take it easy," Karl said as he walked towards him from the side. "She didn't do anything. She just doesn't want you doing anything you're going to regret later. I got some good shit from Snake. How about we all sample it and chill a bit. Leave Jesse hang upside down, but let's just relax and consecrate about a reasonable punishment."

"I think you meant to say 'contemplate,' not 'consecrate,'" Sue Ellen automatically corrected him.

"Huh?"

Harley looked between the two before releasing his finger from the saw trigger and lowering it to his side. Sue Ellen and Karl exchanged a nervous glance, then looked at Harley with hopeful, pleading expressions.

Harley started to laugh, then stopped, and said, "Consecrate? Karl you really are one stupid son-of-a-bitch. Consecrate, seriously?" Harley couldn't contain himself any longer as he started to laugh uncontrollably, almost maniacally.

Karl didn't think his grammar mistake was that funny but forced himself to laugh a little. Sue Ellen couldn't resist and started to giggle. Jesse now regained full consciousness, and when realizing his predicament asked, "What's so fucking funny?"

Sue Ellen, relieved the threat was over, began to relax and laughed all the harder. "I got to go pee before I piss myself," she said, giggling all the way across the room to the bathroom.

Once she was inside and shut the door, Harley, still laughing a little, looked at Karl and ordered him to grab Jesse's left arm and pull it away from his body. Karl did so. Harley told Jesse to extend his pinky finger. Jesse, now noticing that Harley was holding a Sawzall, protested, "No fucking way!"

"Suit yourself," Harley said, "but if you don't do it, I'll take your whole hand off! First you kill a Census worker on our property, then you take a joy-ride in a stolen car in daylight and get in a chase with the state boys! Now stick out your fucking finger cause you need something to remind you not to be so damn stupid!"

Jesse could tell by Harley's tone and demeanor that he was serious. "Please, brother. I'm sorry. I won't do anything stupid ever again. I swear," he begged.

"I know you won't, 'cause now you'll know there are serious consequences to stupid actions that jeopardize all of us. Now stick out your fucking finger!" Harley ordered.

Jesse looked frantically at Karl but knew he wasn't going to get any sympathy from him as he appeared to be enjoying it. Jesse reluctantly extended his pinky and closed his eyes.

Karl activated the Sawzall and deftly severed the pinky from his hand, just below the knuckle. Blood sprayed from the wound onto Karl.

Sue Ellen had just exited the bathroom; her scream wasn't nearly as loud as Jesse's. Harley told Karl to hold Jesse's hand upward to slow the bleeding while he calmly strolled over to the tool bench and sat the Sawzall down. He returned with a small metal hose clamp and a screwdriver. He slipped the hose clamp on the little stump that remained of Jesse's finger and tightened it down with a screwdriver until the bleeding slowed to a drip. Jesse was hyperventilating and tears were streaming down his face.

"Man the fuck up," Harley said. "It was just your pinky finger. Karl, get some of that vodka from the fridge and douse his finger in it. We don't need it getting infected." Karl did as instructed. He returned with a bottle of Stolichnaya fresh from the garage freezer.

"Not the fucking good stuff! That shit's expensive. Grab the bottle of Popov," Harley complained.

Karl did as told and then poured a liberal amount over Jesse's injury.

Harley walked back to his workbench, fired up a handheld Bernzomatic torch, and returned to Jesse. Karl was still holding his hand. Jesse stared at him wild-eyed like a cornered raccoon. "It's okay. I'm just going to cauterize your wound. It's going to hurt like hell, but it needs to be done. Hold him steady, Karl," Harley ordered.

"Wait!" Sue Ellen hollered. "We need to rinse that alcohol off the rest of his hand. It'll be like lighting gasoline otherwise," she warned.

"Damn, I didn't think of that. Good idea. Get some water and a rag to wipe it off."

After Sue Ellen did so, Harley turned up the torch flame, which went from blue to almost white. "Hold him tight, Karl."

"Just fucking do it already!" Jesse snarled.

"Stop!" Sue Ellen yelled once again.

"What now?" Harley asked with impatience.

Sue Ellen looked at Karl and Harley, then settled her gaze on Jesse. She had an odd look on her face, Jesse thought. "Can I do it?" she asked with a gleam in her eye.

Harley shrugged then handed her the torch, "Sure. But make sure you sear it all around real good."

Sue Ellen nodded her head in understanding. "It's going to be okay, Jesse," she assured him as she quickly lowered the flame onto his wound.

Jesse screamed in misery. It was all Karl could do to hold his hand steady as he tried to yank it away and he bucked his body frantically against the chains. The sickening, unmistakable odor of burning human flesh filled the garage. Sue Ellen continued to apply the flame to the stump that was rapidly charring.

Harley and Karl both saw the obvious pleasure displayed on Sue Ellen's face as she continued to torch Jesse's wound. They exchanged concerned glances with each other before Harley finally said, "That's enough,"

Sue Ellen pulled the torch away from Jesse's hand and licked her upper lip. Harley took it from her and turned it off. Jesse had passed out from the intense pain. Harley walked over to the sink and returned with a cup of water. He poured it over

Jesse's wound. The metal hose clamp sizzled, and steam rose from it.

"Lower him on down. He should be good to go. I'm heading back to work. If at least one of these cars ain't parted out by the time I get back this evening, Jesse won't be the only one missing a piece of him. You all got that?"

Karl and Sue Ellen both nodded their heads in unison as Harley walked out of the garage.

CHAPTER 33

The Manning brothers gathered in the cabin's spacious living room around the fieldstone fireplace. A huge 10-point buck's head was mounted at the top. Its glass eyes seemed to stare at each of them. The split pine logs were engulfed by golden and red flames that seemed to hypnotize the brothers as they gazed within. Everyone except Mitch was soaked and cold from the drenching rains that put an early end to their evening hunt. Instead of cold beer, they sipped hot coffee spiked with Buffalo Trace from a variety of mismatched mugs.

"It sounds like a panic attack to me, bro. I've had my share of them over the years," Troy said after Preacher finished telling them all about his experience. Troy did not share with them the nightmare he experienced on the flight to Michigan, or the strong sense of foreboding after waking, as he didn't want to leave. Sure, it was a rough start to a normally great week, but he hoped it would get better. Besides, he wasn't in any rush to return to his world, which was even scarier. The DiCarlo Brothers would get their creditor's money one way or another. Troy was in no hurry to return.

Preacher vigorously shook his head. "I've never experienced anything like this before. It was a visceral feeling. I firmly believe that God was warning me to get all of us out of here."

Mitch sighed before speaking, "I'm not leaving. We get one chance to do this once a year. I agree, it's been a weird camp to say the least, but I'm not leaving."

"I'm with Mitch. Sorry, Preacher, but I look forward to this hunt and time with you guys. Besides, when have we ever run from a problem? Rednecks, weird animals, we can handle anything together, bro," Ryan said.

Troy chimed in, "Hell yes, I'm not going anywhere. Screw these bunch of backwoods freaks."

Now it was Preacher's turn to sigh heavily. "Okay. Obviously, I'm not going to leave you guys, but I'm asking all of you to be extra vigilant. I'm 100 percent certain I was being warned. Something evil is here. If you believe in God, you have to believe in Satan as well. The book of Peter tells us to be alert and sober-minded as our enemy, the devil, prowls around like a roaring lion looking for someone to devour."

The other three brothers nodded, knowing better than to argue with Preacher when he started quoting scripture.

"Maybe not an actual lion, but possibly a Dogman," Ryan mumbled.

"I had the distinct feeling that it wasn't an animal we had to worry about, but rather people," Preacher replied.

"We are animals, bro. If you don't think so, come do a ride-along with me on a weekend night shift," Mitch offered.

"Enough of this worrying and negativity. It's bar night! Let's have a good time. I'm looking forward to some smoked wings, cold beer, and kicking your collective asses at pool," Troy said, trying to change the subject.

"I'm down with that," replied Ryan. "Let's roll."

CHAPTER 34

K arl and Jesse worked on dismantling the Shelby first. Jesse wasn't feeling too bad, mainly because of the Oxycontin, and he had a small stash of coke that Karl didn't know about. It gave him the energy boost he needed. They worked mostly in awkward silence, Jesse still pissed at Karl for not intervening to save his finger and Karl still upset about Jesse taking off with Sue Ellen.

At 5:30, Sue Ellen brought their dinner to the garage: two heaping bowls of wild game stew. It was one of her specialties that included stewed rabbit, squirrel, and venison with chunks of carrots, potatoes, onion, and a host of fresh herbs that she had personally grown. She layered it all on top of fresh biscuits, not the crap from the cardboard tubes. "Take a break and eat some dinner," she said while setting the bowls down on the long workbench. "I made wild game stew."

The brothers stopped what they were doing and sauntered over to the workbench. Jesse eagerly grabbed a bowl and walked to the far end of the bench to eat it. Karl did the same.

"Thanks," Karl muttered as he walked to the fridge and grabbed two bottles of Busch Light. As a small peace offering, he set one before Jesse before sitting down at the opposite end of the bench.

Jesse gave an almost imperceptible nod as he shoveled in the stew. "This is excellent, babe," he said to Sue Ellen.

Karl cringed at Jesse calling Sue Ellen 'babe' but kept it to himself. "It sure is," he agreed.

"Thanks. I'm glad you guys like it. I need to head into work now so I'm taking the Gator. Do you think you'll be by later? It's wing night."

"I doubt it. We haven't even started on my Explorer yet," Karl replied.

"Okay, I'll bring some home for y'all, if I don't see you guys later."

Karl watched her leave the garage, wondering if he had lost her to Jesse.

• • • •

• • • •

HARLEY RETURNED HOME at 9 o'clock. Jesse and Karl were just finishing up the Shelby. "Nice work. I'm going to grab a shower. After that, let's head over to the bar. It's wing night. I'm picking up the tab," he said.

Karl and Jesse, both dumbfounded, watched him leave. Harley only picked up a tab on their birthdays or holidays. Besides, the Explorer was parked in the next bay in full view. Both figured they would be working most of the night and into the morning to finish up, as he had ordered them to do earlier.

Jesse looked at Karl after Harley left. Karl shrugged and said, "Hell if I know. Maybe he got laid."

CHAPTER 35

L The Black Bear Tavern was a typical quaint northern Michigan bar. It was situated on the bank of the Au Sable River. The outside wasn't much to look at, about the same size as an average ranch-style home with a barnlike exterior. Gray smoke curled from a small metal chimney sticking out of the roof.

The large windows that faced the road were covered with a huge banner that read "Welcome Deer Hunters." One small neon sign featuring Pabst beer on draft, with both of the e's burned out, was in the other window, alongside a "We Sell Lottery" sign and a handful of other beer posters.

Mitch steered his Suburban into the small gravel lot out front, deftly dodging the numerous puddles from the earlier storm. He drove to the far end of the lot and backed into an empty area. A dozen or so other trucks and a few ATVs caked with mud were scattered about. He shifted into park and turned off the engine, then handed the keys to Preacher and said, "You're driving back."

"I would hope so. I'm only planning on having a couple. I know you boys will triple that."

"At least," Troy added from the backseat.

As Troy and Ryan started to pop open their rear doors, Mitch said, "Hold on a sec, guys."

Each stopped and looked inquiringly at Mitch.

"If either of you are carrying, hand 'em over. We are not mixing excessive booze with bullets tonight."

146

Ryan nodded his head in agreement and surrendered his Sig Sauer 9mm to Mitch.

"I'm not so sure it's a wise idea going in there without someone being gun-upped. Especially with the problems we already had with some locals and Preacher's warning... Um, feeling... Or whatever it was," Troy said.

"I agree. That's why Preacher will be carrying. He's only having a couple brews. I'm leaving mine locked up inside as well," Mitch said, holding out his hand to Troy.

Troy sighed and mumbled "whatever," then handed over the compact Taurus 9mm he had borrowed from Ryan.

"Relax. I've always got your six. It'll be fine, brothers; just enjoy the evening,"

Preacher said, projecting more positivity than he felt.

"Any more damn rules?" Troy asked with irritation.

"Yeah. Don't screw anyone's wife or girlfriend!" Mitch added sternly.

Preacher was carrying his Bersa Firestorm .380. He had the flush-fit magazine that held 7 rounds in the magazine plus one in the barrel. Mitch usually gave him shit about it being a "girly" gun, but Preacher liked the easy concealability of it and loved the way it fit his hand. He wasn't an expert with it or any handgun, but he was a decent shot. Most people that knew him as a Deacon were surprised that he had a concealed weapons permit.

Mitch popped the hatch and secured the guns into a custom-built safe he had installed. He secured the safe and the SUV. They trooped towards the door, stepping carefully around the puddles. Bob Seger's "Ramblin' Gamblin' Man" could be heard from within. Stars were just starting to peek through the gaps in the quickly passing clouds overhead.

The brothers bunched up at the door, as they always did at a strange northern bar. No one wanted to be first in, as that person drew the stares of everyone within, and most of the time the locals didn't smile. In some of the bars, the overwhelming sense of hostility was so much that they simply left after one beer. Locals were protective of their watering holes.

"I'll do it," Mitch said, even though no one had spoken. "It can't be any worse than a night shift when I'm called by the bar owner to toss out a few drunk-as-skunks patrons that don't want to leave."

"Except you're not in uniform, and you don't have any weapons with you," Troy observed.

"Come on, bro, I am a weapon," Mitch replied jokingly as he yanked open the door and stepped inside.

He surveyed the interior as all cops do with a quick glance of everything and everyone inside. It looked casual but was a comprehensive threat assessment for both action and evasion if necessary. The first thing he saw was a squatty guy about Preacher's age, giving him a hard stare. He was wearing a sleeveless leather biker vest and was leaning over the pool table to the immediate left of the door about to break a fresh rack. He paused when Mitch entered and glared at him as though he had walked into his own home unannounced.

Mitch ignored the stare and surveilled the remainder of the interior. One intoxicated couple occupied a cramped dance floor to the left of the bar near a classic Wurlitzer jukebox. They clung to each other as though slow dancing, but by the looks of things were probably just supporting each other from falling over.

Four men and one woman sat on well-worn barstools directly across the room from the entrance door with their backs to him. Despite this, each of them had their eyes fixed on Mitch and his entourage in the large mirror behind the bar. The men's expressions were neutral, but the lone woman smiled at him.

A cluster of tables and chairs to the right comprised the small dining area. Three sets of older couples occupied them and were eagerly gnawing on plump chicken wings. They paid little attention to him. Mitch noticed sliding glass doors that led to a rear deck area that was lined with a strand of single bare lightbulbs dangling from the exterior overhead porch. It appeared empty, most likely, he figured, due to the recent passing storm and subsequent cooler air it had brought with it.

The interior was in a lot nicer shape than the exterior and it lived up to its name. An entire bearskin rug was splayed out above the jukebox on the wall. A full-size taxidermied black bear stood menacingly to the right of the bar. Its mouth wide was open in a snarl, revealing long incisors, and huge claws protruded from its front paws that were held upward in front of it. Huge metal foot-hold bear traps hung from behind the bar, dangling by their iron chains. A classic black and white framed photo of the legendary Michigan bowman, Fred Bear, posing over an enormous black bear he arrowed, was the centerpiece of the dining area's wall.

Mitch quickly decided that besides the biker at the pool table, the bar's atmosphere seemed fairly neutral—at least as neutral as an "Up North" bar could be to strangers. He led the way to a couple of small vacant high-top tables in the left corner behind the pool table. He liked his back in a corner with a view of anything approaching; besides, they had come to play pool as well as eat and drink. The place smelled of chicken wings, beer, and damp clothes.

The biker's eyes followed Mitch and his brothers until they walked behind him. He then returned his attention to the table and slammed the pool ball with terrific force into the other balls. They went flying in a multitude of directions when the cue ball exploded into them. Three of them found holes to fall into. The biker straightened and turned towards the brothers, and asked, "Table's open. Any takers or do I keep playing solo cause everyone else in here are a bunch of pussies?"

The other Manning brothers all looked towards the best pool player among them.

Preacher held his hands palm up and shook his head. "No way. I'm just here to have some wings and a couple of beers."

Preacher had worked at a pool hall in the north end of Toledo, after school and on Saturdays for most of his high school years. During that time, he learned the game and quickly excelled at it, especially under the tutelage of the owner at the time, who was the first cousin of Minnesota Fats. After enlisting in the Army, Preacher continued to hone his skills at many bars and taverns across the country. He rarely lost, and many superior officers were in his debt across a variety of Army bases.

"Tell you what," the biker said. "You beat me, and I'll buy you and all your buddies all the wings and beer you all can drink! And if I beat you, well, then, you only owe me a beer."

"Come on, Preacher. You can't beat those odds," Troy remarked.

"You got this, Preacher. Live a little," Ryan encouraged.

"Do what you want, Preacher. No pressure, brother," Mitch chimed in.

Preacher shrugged off his camo jacket and hung it behind a chair, then selected a stick from the rack in the corner, shaking his head at its pitiful condition. He grabbed a cube of blue chalk and dabbed it about the tip. When satisfied, he looked at Mitch and said, "Grab me a draft of Bud."

The biker smiled crookedly, revealing teeth that probably rarely saw a brush, let alone a dentist chair. He was squatty, bald, and had a snow-white bushy Fu Manchu style mustache. His tattooed upper arms were the size of small tree trunks. "Finally! Someone with some balls in this place," he said.

"Speaking of balls, you knocked in two solids and a stripe. It's still your shot," Preacher remarked.

The biker nodded and lined up a long shot at another solid. He made it but missed the next one. Preacher analyzed the table, walking all around it. He paused here and there while leaning his head one way or the other. At times he knelt and reviewed the angles like a golfer in preparation for a long putt.

"Come on! What the fuck? Are you playing chess or pool?" the biker griped, and looked back at the other patrons with a 'can you believe this guy' expression.

Preacher ignored him and finally lined up a difficult bank for an across-side shot and easily made it. He sunk the next five with equal ease, despite half the shots being extremely difficult. He paused and took a swig of the beer Mitch had delivered, then surveyed the eight-ball. It was tight against the middle of the far rail and sandwiched between two solids, with the cue ball resting against the opposite rail directly across from it. Most of the guys at the bar and the lone woman, who Mitch had learned was the barmaid, were now off their chairs, intently watching the match with awe.

"You're screwed. You got no shot. Lucky run, but it's over now," the biker remarked with glee.

"I would double or nothing on this shot, but how do you double all the wings and beer we can eat and drink?" Preacher asked him.

The biker opened his hands wide, shook his head, and said, "Name it, whatever you want."

Preacher took a long drink of his draft before saying, "I want you to attend a church service tomorrow."

The biker screwed up his already ugly face, scrunching his nose and half-closing his eyes as though physically pained. "You serious?"

"As a heart attack. And, you have to stay for the entire service," Preacher replied.

"You a damn pastor or something?"

"Or something," Preacher answered.

The biker laughed and said, "You got it, Father. Let's see your shit, cause you ain't got a chance in hell of making that shot."

"Yeah, well, maybe I got a chance in Heaven of making it," Preacher said as he tapped the corner pocket to his right. "It'll be off the four ball," he said as he powered the cue ball smoothly across the felt, striking the 8-ball just a tad to the left of its center. It smashed against the 4-ball before racing across the green, then back towards Preacher at a diagonal before depositing itself into the corner pocket.

Preacher's brothers and the other onlookers cheered wildly. The biker stared in disbelief.

Just then, two men that looked an awful lot like the biggest of the Duck Dynasty Brothers entered the tavern, followed by a man that made them both look small. He appeared to be of Native American ancestry and had a face that could only be described as badly in need of a fist.

Ryan couldn't believe it. It was the same two guys that were riding his ass on the way up to the cabin just yesterday and had practically run him and Troy off the road. How many assholes lived in the area? he wondered. Now all they needed was the two rednecks that almost hit him and Mitch yesterday evening to stop by.

As if on cue, those same two rednecks entered the door. Ryan was in total disbelief. It was a completely surreal moment. He glanced at Mitch and realized he was thinking the same thing.

CHAPTER 36

Harley was driving his tow truck, with Jesse stuck in the middle and Karl on the passenger side. "I told Snake we were going for wings. He's going to meet us there. The Buford brothers were visiting him when I called so they're tagging along too," Harley said, then asked, "You and Snake going to be okay together?"

"Yeah. We're good," Karl answered, then added, "Should be some decent pool games with the Bufords coming."

"Careful, Karl. Them boys took you good last month," said Harley.

"They got lucky was all. I was fucked up by the time they showed up. I wasn't even on my game."

"Well, play 'em early this time before you get too messed up."

Karl nodded his head. Jesse flexed his left hand. He had removed the hose clamp earlier and Sue Ellen had wrapped the stub with gauze and tape. He grimaced at the pain but the oxy was keeping it tolerable. Karl noticed this and said to Harley, "I may need you as a partner. Jesse probably ain't up to it."

"I can play," Jesse interjected.

"Course you can, it was only your little finger," Harley added, as he steered the wrecker into the lot and parked next to a black Suburban.

"Son of a bitch!" Karl said.

"It's them," Jesse added.

Harley looked questioningly at them.

"The Suburban. That's the assholes that almost hit us yes-terday," Karl replied while pointing at the SUV.

Jesse wasn't about to add that he cut their tires earlier, let alone tell him that the same guys had seen him and Karl in the stolen Shelby. Who knew how Harley would react?

"That's a hell of a coincidence," Harley said, "Not only be-cause you had a run-in with them, but that I towed them into my shop earlier because someone had punctured all their tires while they were hunting this morning."

"Uh. We didn't have anything to do with that. I mean, I sure didn't," Karl replied while now looking at Jesse.

Jesse could feel the pressure from both his brothers staring at him. He knew Harley could tell when he was lying. "Sue Ellen did it," he only half lied.

"Sue Ellen?" Karl said with obvious doubt.

"Now why the hell would she do that?" asked Harley.

"Yeah, why would she do that?" Karl added with skepti-cism.

"Don't act all innocent about this, Karl. Why don't you tell Harley."

"Tell me what? What the fuck is going on?"

"Two guys that were in that Suburban saw us in the Shelby yesterday morning while we were driving it back to the barn. The same two from the night before that almost hit us." Jesse said.

Harley interlaced his hands behind his head and let out a long sigh. Karl scowled at Jesse. "Why, for fuck's sake, am I just hearing about this now?" Harley asked in a low, even-mannered tone. When no one answered, he slammed his right fist onto the dash. "Dammit, someone better answer me!" He yelled.

"Because we knew you would be pissed. Just like you are now!" Jesse said while looking down at the floor, knowing that Harley had a murderous gaze fixed on him. A solitary tear leaked from Jesse's eye, then several more. "Please don't hurt me anymore, Harley. I'm sorry. I'm so fucking stupid. If you want, I'll leave. I'll move out, just don't hurt me no more," he begged.

Harley was taken aback. He never saw Jesse shed a tear before. He suddenly felt remorse for cutting off his finger. Jesse was just a kid, barely an adult. Harley put his arm around Jesse's shoulders and said, "It's okay, brother. I'm sorry for cutting off your finger. That was wrong. Hell, you're practically still a kid. Besides, you're fucked up in the head a bit. I'm not going to hurt you anymore."

Jesse looked up from the floor and wiped his cheeks dry with the back of his hand, surprised at the sincerity in Harley's voice. "Thanks, Harley. I'm really sorry."

"I know you is. And no more talk of moving out."

Headlights bounced across the lot as a truck pulled in. Harley saw that it was the Buford brothers' pickup. "Jesse, you go on and get out. I want to talk to Karl alone a minute. The Buford's just pulled in. I'm sure Snake is with 'em. Go on over and ask them to wait for me before they head in."

Karl suddenly felt nauseated. He opened the door and hopped out to let Jesse get past him. After he did so, he slowly climbed back in the truck and turned to face Harley.

"Is all he said true?" asked Harley.

Karl cleared his throat and started to talk, but immediately began stuttering. Harley slapped him hard across the face. The power of the blow turned his head sideways. "Don't you fucking lie to me!" Harley snarled.

Karl was having a really bad couple days: getting shot at, having his gal stolen from him by his little brother, and getting beat on by Snake. All those things probably caused him to react as he did. Since he never stood up to his older brother before, it caught Harley totally off guard.

Karl pulled his snub nose .357 Smith & Wesson revolver from his rear waistband and drove it hard into Harley's lower jaw as though delivering an uppercut. He held it in place while Harley started to gag and pulled back the trigger. "You ain't the boss of me, brother. I'm so fucking tired of you acting like you are. Yes, what Jesse said is true. The guys in that Suburban saw us in the Shelby but they didn't see where we went with it or follow us. I didn't think it was a problem, but knew you would overreact like you always do." Spittle sprayed from Karl's mouth as he vehemently hissed out the words.

"Easy, brother, don't accidentally pull that trigger. Is Sue Ellen messing with your mind? I mean, fighting Snake and now this?"

"Leave her out of this. I'm just tired of you thinking you're king shit. Ever since Dad died, you been acting like the boss of us. We're equals. You want to boss folks around then get yourself a wife and kids, but back the fuck off me! Understand?"

"Dammit, Karl, take it down a couple of gears. You is lookin like you really want to pull that trigger. We're brothers. You and Jesse is all I got left. I'm sorry if I've been an overbearing asshole. I'm just trying to keep us all together and out of prison," Harley pleaded.

Karl withdrew the gun from the underside of Harley's jaw. He slowly let the trigger back with his thumb. Harley exhaled a long steady breath and rubbed his jaw. He was beyond shocked at what just happened. He was silent a few seconds before saying, "Okay, brother. Let's huddle up with Jesse, Massey, and the Buford brothers and figure out how we are going to handle these assholes that saw you in the Shelby." Harley then reached under his seat, retrieved his pistol, and tucked it in his ankle holster. "It's a damn shame. Those boys I towed in today seemed like nice guys."

A few minutes later, after devising a plan and sharing some meth with Massey and the Bufords, Harley said, "Let's do this. I mean, if that's okay with you Karl?"

Karl straightened up a notch. His brother was checking with him before moving forward with a plan. Apparently, their talk in the wrecker did some good. Karl felt supercharged. The meth had fired him up even more. Hell, Karl thought, he felt like Doc Holliday getting ready to kick some ass, like in that movie Jessie loved.

"Sounds good. You got the back covered, Harley?"

"I sure do, bro. They try to come out that back patio and they'll have to get by me."

Karl looked at the rest of the group. "Okay. Let's do this. Remember, don't hurt Sue Ellen by accident. Now let's go and show them out-of-town boys what backwoods justice feels like."

CHAPTER 37

"**P**reacher, there is going to be trouble soon. Don't draw that pistol unless you fully intend to use it," Mitch turned and whispered to his eldest brother after seeing the group enter the bar.

Troy, who was flirting with the barmaid, now also noticed who had entered. He leaned close to her ear and whispered, "You may want to call 911. The guys that just came in are going to cause problems."

"Those boys are regulars. You'll be fine, honey, just don't fuck with them," Sue Ellen replied and walked towards the group.

It might be too late for that, he thought. Troy watched as Sue Ellen hugged two of them and guided them all to the bar, except the huge Native American-looking guy with the black ponytail who sat at a small high-top near the entrance door. The three guys that were already sitting at the bar grabbed their drinks and popped up from their stools as though they were caught sneaking seats in a reserved section of a ball game. The others took their stools. Sue Ellen filled a pitcher with Busch Light and placed it before them. She distributed frosted mugs, then filled one from the tap, which she carried over to Snake. All five kept glancing over at the Manning brothers while sipping their drafts.

"Is there a problem, Karl?" The biker asked one of the men. "Why do you and your posse keep looking at me?"

"No problem with you, Hank," Karl replied.

The biker looked at Mitch and his brothers and asked, "You all got a beef with them boys?"

Mitch shook his head and said, "Not that I know of, but we have bumped into them on a couple of occasions the last two days, and someone sliced all my tires on my Suburban this morning." Mitch looked steadily at Karl when he answered.

Hank looked between Mitch and Karl and said in a half-whisper to Mitch, "Don't push 'em. They are crazy-ass inbreds. Just ignore them and you should be fine."

Mitch nodded his head, as did Preacher.

"It's all yours," the biker said to Preacher while gesturing at the pool table. "That was a hell of a game you shot. I know when I'm out of my league."

"Thanks, but I'm done. I'll see you at noon mass tomorrow."

"I honor my bets. I'll be there but hopefully, I don't cause an earthquake or something else catastrophic," The biker, now known as Hank, replied with a grin.

"Me and my friend challenge you and whoever you want for a partner," Karl said to Preacher while walking over to the table with one of the Buford brothers tailing him.

"Table's all yours. I'm done," Preacher replied.

"Fuck that. I challenged you. Pick a partner," Karl said, trying to sound stern.

"Listen, son. I don't take orders from anyone since I retired from the Army. Like I said, I'm done," Preacher replied with a bit of edge to his voice.

"I don't think you understand how things work here," Karl replied as he inserted the two quarters and jammed the lever in, releasing the pool balls with a rumble as they tumbled down the track.

Hank spoke up, "The man said he doesn't want to play. That ain't too hard to understand even for you, is it, Karl?"

"I suggest you hit the road, Hank," answered Karl.

"I suggest you go fuck yourself," Hank replied evenly.

Karl glanced back at the Buford brothers and Snake as if seeking guidance. Snake just smiled and the Buford brothers looked at him blankly. Jesse snickered a little. "Look, Hank. I don't want any trouble with you, but I suggest you leave now. This ain't your business, okay?"

The Manning brothers were watching the exchange with interest. Mitch was sensing they may have an unlikely ally. Jesse shoved Karl aside and started towards the biker. "You heard what my brother said, old man. Get the hell out of here before I fuck you up," he said while producing a Gerber pocket knife that he quickly flicked open, revealing a 4" stainless steel blade.

Hank grabbed the narrow end of his cue stick that was resting on the table and swung it back-handed across his body, connecting it with the side of Jesse's head. The resulting "thwack" caused everyone inside to wince except for Jesse, who let out an "augh" as his eyes rolled upwards and he crumpled to the floor.

The remaining patrons that were eating in the dining area now hurriedly dropped money on their tables and started for the exit. The three guys that were watching the pool game also gulped down their beers and threw money on the bar before heading out quickly, as though someone pulled a fire alarm.

The Manning brothers exchanged glances among each other, sizing up their situation and their odds. Mitch thought they were about 50/50, especially with the biker as an ally, but the

Native American-looking guy and the Buford brothers were huge. The three of them looked like they belonged on the WWE circuit.

Karl now pulled back his flannel shirt, revealing the butt end of his snub nose .357 revolver. Preacher started to go for his gun, but Mitch grabbed his hand and shook his head. He then yelled, "That's enough," and raised his hands in front of him, slowly walking sideways between the biker and Karl. "What is it that you want with us?"

"I can handle this inbred asshole," Hank complained as he stepped over the unconscious Jesse and started to walk around Mitch.

"It isn't worth anyone dying over. Just let us talk with them," stated Mitch.

Ryan grabbed an empty glass beer mug from the adjacent table and Troy was fingering his knife on his belt underneath his shirt.

Hank chuckled. "You don't know these boys like I do. They ain't gonna talk with ya. If you got beef with them they'll kill ya outright and then feed ya to their hogs. These here boys are sick little puppies. You all seem decent enough to me, but if you want out of here, you're going to have to fight your way out. If you don't, you're as good as dead anyway. In fact, I just saw on the news earlier there is a missing Census worker that was supposed to be in our area. I wouldn't be the least surprised that Karl and his dipshit brothers are involved with that. Ain't that right, Karl?"

"No, it ain't. None of that is right, Hank. Why are you telling such tall tales? We just want to shoot some pool. Jesse probably had that comin' for charging ya like he did, so I'll overlook it this one time. Now put that pool stick down on the table and go ahead and run along."

"Tell you what. I'll be his partner, and when we beat you, these here gentlemen get to walk on out of here without any problem."

Karl nodded his head and said, "And if we win, you give me that vest of yours."

Hank knew if he gave up his vest he was as good as dead with his gang because the number one rule was to never give up your colors. Truth be told, the gang was thinning, and not just their hair. The "Logger" gang was down to seven members from 27 back in their prime during the early seventies. Their youngest member was 59 now, and the oldest 71. But, Hank reasoned, he just witnessed a guy run the table against him and figured they were a sure win. He knew Karl was a damn good pool player, but this visitor was on another level. He accepted the bet.

Mitch encouraged Preacher to do the same, hoping that maybe they could walk out of the bar instead of having to fight, or worse, shoot their way out.

Preacher had Hank break. The balls dispersed weakly; none fell but two stripes landed squarely in front of pockets. Karl smiled. His loose, but not too loose to be obvious, rack had worked in his favor. Hank bitched about the rack, but Karl ignored him and quickly sank the two easy shots before knocking in a long third one. He missed on his fourth one, a cross-side bank.

Troy bought his brothers a round of beers and a shot of Jack, and bought the same for Hank, their new biker friend. Preacher declined the shot, but Hank gladly downed it, as well as his own. Mitch thought it best to stay clear-headed and ignored the shot but sipped his beer.

Preacher sank four straight balls, two of them practically impossible shots, but his fifth shot was a tad light and stranded the ball just on the edge of a corner pocket.

Jesse finally started to regain consciousness. He was moaning and squirming on the floor. Sue Ellen had placed a cold towel on his forehead and was slapping his cheek lightly. The other Buford brother, not in the game, helped him to his feet. Jesse glared at Hank while rubbing the side of his head, and asked Sue Ellen for a beer. He staggered over to the bar and she gave him a towel filled with ice to hold against his head, as well as a tall draft.

The Buford boy was good. He ran the table down to the 8-ball but missed a long opposite corner bank shot. Hank sank the next three but made an amateurish mistake and scratched on the 8-ball. His face went pale.

Karl whooped and hollered and said, "Surrender the booty," while holding out his hand. Hank shook his head while slowly shrugging off the leather vest and handing it to Karl.

The Manning brothers finished their beers and now exchanged worried glances. Hank's head was bowed, and his shoulders slumped, making him look every bit like a beatdown dog.

"Don't worry, Hank. I'm gonna give it back to you. I know how important these things are to you guys," Karl said. Hank straightened up a bit upon hearing that.

"But first, I'm thinking Jesse here might want to piss all over it."

Jesse smiled widely as Karl threw the jacket to him. He caught it then stood up from the barstool and tossed the jacket on the floor. He unzipped his pants and started to urinate on it.

Hank started to scramble around the pool table but the Buford brothers each grabbed an arm and held him back as Jesse emptied the contents of his bladder onto the jacket. When finished, he zipped up and said, "It's all yours, old man."

Hank was like a rabid dog. He let loose with a volley of profanities and expletives that should not have gone together but somehow related his feelings. Spittle flew from his mouth and Mitch had to help restrain him. He finally tired and quit struggling.

"Now go git your jacket and git out. We is going to have a private chat with these friends of yours," Karl said as he pulled out his .357 snub nose and rested it against his thigh.

"You best not kill them. I swear I'll come after you if you do. This ain't over between us, Karl!" Hank said with a snarl.

"I suspect it ain't, but git going before I'm not in such a cheerable mood."

"I think you meant 'charitable,'" Sue Ellen piped up but immediately regretted it.

"What the fuck ever! Cheerable, charitable, who gives two shits, Sue Ellen!" Karl said with dismay.

The Bufordss released Hank, who walked over to the bar. Sue Ellen handed him a garbage bag. He took it while scowling at Jesse and scooped his jacket up in it, then ambled towards the front door. Snake stood from his stool with his arms folded, shaking his head.

"Use the back exit," Karl said while pointing towards the rear sliders that led to the patio.

Hank turned and walked that way. At the rear door, he glanced back at Preacher and said, "I'll be in church tomorrow. Like I said. I honor my bets."

Preacher nodded and Hank headed out the door.

Karl looked at the Manning brothers and said, "We is all going for a little ride."

Mitch looked at Karl and said, "Whatever needs to be said can be said here."

Two loud clicks sounded behind the Manning brothers. Mitch knew the unmistakable sound of a double-barrel shotgun's hammers being cocked back, as did his brothers. "I suggest you boys do what Karl says."

The Manning brothers looked behind them to see the cute barmaid leveling a Colt 12-gauge side by side sawed-off shotgun towards them. Troy looked at her with surprise and alarm.

"Like you said, them boys were going to be trouble, but so am, I sweetheart," she said with a wink.

CHAPTER 38

Harley was getting anxious. He told Karl to go inside and clear out the bar of everyone except the tourists. He didn't want a public spectacle with witnesses. It was doubtful that any of the locals would talk as they all knew better, but he didn't want to take that chance.

Twenty minutes later, when Hank, the last of the locals, finally exited out the back, Harley wasn't happy. He knew Hank well and didn't want to kill him.

Hank looked startled to see Harley leaning against the deck rail with an AR-15 resting against it as well. "Damn! I didn't see you there. Are you expecting some kind of war?" Hank said while looking at the rifle.

"I hope not, but it's better to be prepared for any eventuality. What's in the bag?"

Hank looked at the bag then at Harley. "Don't get me started, Harley. Your fucking dumbass brothers are starting shit again and it appears you are too. I'm not sure why you are targeting those guys but y'all better think this through. Four guys disappear a couple of days after a Census worker goes missing; this area will be crawling with cops the likes you've never seen before. You want that, Harley?"

"I don't know nothin' 'bout the Census guy. Folks get lost all the time around here."

"Horseshit, Harley. I know what you and your brothers are capable of, everyone does around here, but five guys disappear within a few days of each other and you'll have every news out-

167

let and police jurisdiction including the FBI up your ass. Think about it."

And that is exactly what Harley did. It was the only reason he let Hank walk away. He was thinking that getting questioned about a stolen car by the state police was a hell of a lot better than getting questioned about the disappearance of several brothers, and a local. Hell, he might even make an anonymous tip against Karl. It might do him some good to be locked up a couple of years, especially with the stunt he pulled in the truck. Who the hell did he think he was? It was time to reel-in the initial plan. Nobody was abducting and killing anyone over the stolen car.

Harley stashed the rifle in his truck and strode in the back door. He saw Karl pointing a handgun at four guys, two of them he had met earlier. Sue Ellen had a double-barrel shotgun leveled at them and was screaming something about blowing them in half if they didn't do what Karl said.

"Shut up, Sue, and both of you put those fucking guns away. What the hell is the matter with you two?" Harley said. He approached Mitch and Ryan. "I apologize for my brother and the barmaid. Fact is, my brother told me that you all had a run in yesterday, and the Buford brothers here supposedly had an incident with y'all as well the day before that. You gots to understand that we are a close-knit community. We handle our own business. We don't trouble any police over minor shit. They got more important things to handle."

"Seems like pointing loaded firearms at folks and threatening to abduct them is a bit more than minor," Mitch replied.

Harley laughed and said, "Sticks and stones. Maybe where you're from, but around here guns are pointed at each other every fucking weekend. You boys choose to come up north, well, this is how we party."

Ryan started to speak up, but Mitch held up his hand and shook his head. Mitch sensed the man was sincere about letting them leave. He would contact the police as soon as they did and have all these rednecks arrested on felonious assault charges as well as attempted kidnapping. "Okay. Apology accepted." Mitch said and grabbed his jacket from the rear of the chair, shrugging it on. "Like you said, no one was hurt."

"Fuck that!" Jesse yelled from the barstool. "My head nearly got cracked open."

"That wasn't us. You know it was that biker, and besides, you came at him with a knife," Preacher said.

Jesse started to speak again but Harley pointed at him and said, "Shut up!"

The other Manning brothers grabbed their jackets as well. Mitch looked at Troy and said, "Tip the lady."

Troy looked incredulously at Mitch and said, "The crazy bitch almost shot us!"

Preacher gave Troy a withering look. He grumbled something then threw ten dollars on the table.

One of the Buford brothers complained to Harley, "The little fuck there ran us off the road day before yesterday," while pointing at Ryan. "If you and your brothers want to make peace, fine, but I want a piece of this little bitch before he leaves here."

"Fuck you, Paul Bunyan! You tried to run us off the road. You want a piece of me, I'll gladly give you the chance. Call me little again and I'll make you cry besides beating your ass," Ryan yelled back.

Harley nodded his head as Mitch shook his. *Aw shit, Ryan's in full Napoleon mode again,* Mitch thought. Preacher said a quick Hail Mary for all of them under his breath, and Troy thought, *Here we go!*

"Use the dance floor. I don't need the owner pissing and moaning about how something got busted in here because of you boys trying to show who has bigger balls," Sue Ellen said.

Ryan took his camo jacket back off and walked to the center of the dance floor. The Buford brother stalked forward, eyeing Ryan like a heavyweight fighter would against a flyweight with bemusement in his eyes. To him, it was a done deal already. Mitch recognized the over-confident look and smiled to himself at the surprise the big guy was about to get.

Being insecure due to his size, Ryan had decided to pursue wrestling in school. Every high school is known for something and Bedford High School in Temperance, Michigan is known for its outstanding wrestling program. Despite being an hour's drive each way from their Adrian home, Ryan attended school there because of their wrestling reputation.

Ryan was the runner-up in his weight class at the state championship in both his junior and senior years. Not satisfied with simply taking people down, he joined a boxing club in the city of Adrian just after graduation. He was a formidable fighter, especially when his infamous temper kicked in.

Ryan started to bounce on his toes and adopted a classic boxer's position. The Buford brother laughed as he stalked forward and launched a left jab at Ryan's face. He easily batted away the jab with his left hand and, while ducking to his left, saw a roundhouse right coming. Ryan leaned away from it. The powerful punch just nicked his chin rather than hit him square on the side of his jaw. Ryan now pivoted quickly to his left while delivering a punishing right to his adversary's exposed ribs. Everyone winced at the sound of the impact. Before he straightened up, Ryan pivoted the opposite direction and pounded a left hook into the back of the big guy's kidneys.

The big man went down to one knee and Ryan jumped on his back, trying to wrap him up in a sleeper hold. He almost had the neck secure when the man suddenly stood up and ran backward, with Ryan clinging to him like a spider monkey. After several strides, he smashed Ryan against the back wall with such force that the entire floor shook. The crash jolted the jukebox which started playing Van Halens's "Jump."

Ryan struggled to regain his breath. The big guy took two huge strides forward with Ryan still on his back. He stopped abruptly and ran backward into the exposed log surface, once again smashing Ryan. He couldn't maintain his grip any longer and slithered to the floor.

"Get up Ryan. Get up!" Troy urged while Mitch and Preacher shouted encouragement as well.

"Finish his punk ass!" Karl yelled to the Buford brother.

The Buford brother turned around and grabbed hold of Ryan's shirt collar, lifting him completely off his feet. He effortlessly spun him around like a shot putter and launched him across the room. Ryan sailed about 12 feet before landing on top of a dining table that crumpled under his weight.

"Watch the damn furniture, you asshole!" Sue Ellen screamed at the Buford brother as he stomped towards Ryan.

Although badly shaken, Ryan was coming around quickly from a massive adrenaline dump but played possum until the big guy was almost to him. When the big guy came into range,

Ryan launched a forward kick into his opponent's stomach. He rolled off the table just as the guy emptied the contents of his stomach onto it. Ryan now grabbed a nearby wooden chair and swung it against the guy's side. It shattered about him like dry kindling wood, but the big guy seemed unfazed. Ryan was unaware that the man's pain was mostly masked by meth.

The Buford brother took a quick step forward and tackled Ryan to the floor. Ryan grinned. He loved the floor. It reminded him of his wrestling days. He quickly spun under the guy onto his stomach, then did a partial pushup as the guy attempted to get a hold of his wrists. Ryan then purposely collapsed to his right side, causing the man to start to roll that way, and, using his momentum, slipped out from under him and scrambled onto the guy's back.

This time before going for the sleeper hold, he hammered his right forearm across the back of the big man's head, bouncing it off the floor beneath him. While he was dazed, Ryan now easily slipped in for the neck hold and began to squeeze his right arm around the guy's neck like a vise. The huge man wildly flailed about and attempted to roll over, but Ryan kept his feet wide apart to prevent that. The guy now launched short punches over his shoulder but wasn't able to connect with any power to Ryan's face or head. In a last-ditch effort, he attempted to push himself up but only made it halfway before collapsing to the floor. Ryan maintained the pressure an additional few seconds to ensure he was unconscious before releasing the hold and shakily standing up.

The other Buford brother started towards Ryan, but Harley quickly stepped into his path and said, "That's enough. He took him down fair and square." The brother glared at Ryan but didn't push past Harley. "Now go check on your brother. Make sure he's okay."

Harley turned to Ryan and said, "You're a scrappy lit..." Harley was about to say 'little' but decided against it, and continued, "fighter. Go ahead and leave, all of ya, but jest remember what happens here in our community is handled by us. I suggest y'all keep the things that happened here to yourselves."

Mitch and his brothers started toward the front door. Snake eyed them all but allowed them to pass.

Once out the door and into the parking lot, the brothers practically ran to the Suburban.

CHAPTER 39

"What kind of bullshit was that?" Karl said as soon as the Manning brothers left the bar. "I thought you said to clear out the bar and secure the tourists. For what?

To let them fuckin' walk! They'll call the cops on us."

"Let 'em. It's their word against all of ours. They got no proof of anything. If we would've killed 'em we would have had all kinds of cops and reporters up our ass. Think about it." Harley said while tapping his temple.

"Well, we could have at least fucked 'em up a bit," Jesse added.

Harley laughed. "That didn't work out so well for Logan, did it?" he said while gesturing to the older of the Buford Brothers, who was still rubbing his neck and had some ice on his ribs. "If they all can fight like that little guy, you and Karl would have gotten your asses kicked."

"I could've taken that kid," Karl said with conviction.

"It's a done deal. Leave it be. Snake and I got some business to take care of in Flint tonight. We'll be gone all night, so y'all best get back home in case the cops do show up here. I'll call Randy and see if he's working. Maybe he can help us out. Sue Ellen, maybe you should close up early. Just call Harold and tell him you're sick and no one is here anyhow. We'll come up with a story to feed to the cops if they happen to call 'em. I'm thinking they're headed to their cabin and changing their shorts about now before packing up and heading back south where they belong."

• • • •

MITCH DROVE THE SUBURBAN out of the bar parking lot and headed towards Mio. Preacher, Ryan, and Troy were all talking excitedly at once. Preacher asked why they were not headed towards the cabin. Ryan asked for the gun safe combo while leaning over the backseat into the cargo area, and Troy said they should gun up and head back to the bar and make a citizen's arrest on the whole bunch.

Mitch, who was keeping an eye on the rearview mirror to ensure no one was following them, suddenly jammed on the brakes and pulled to the side of the road. "That's enough! Everyone relax. We're not going back to have a shootout like the O.K. Corral. I'm taking us to the Sheriff Department in Mio. We'll file a report there," he said.

Ryan was flung forward and bounced off the rear of Mitch's seat when he had suddenly braked.

"Jesus! Easy brother. I was halfway in the cargo hold. I've been fucking flung around enough for one night."

"Watch your mouth." Preacher didn't tolerate taking the Lord's name in vain.

"Sorry," Ryan mumbled.

Mitch gave the safe combination to Ryan and told him to distribute everyone's guns in case they were ambushed on the way. He then resumed driving.

Preacher said he liked the idea of going directly to the police but, once that was done, wanted to pack up and head home immediately. He reminded all of them of his premonition, which thus far seemed to be spot on.

Troy and Ryan protested. Neither wanted to be run off by some rednecks. Mitch suggested that they should at least pack up and head somewhere an hour or so away to avoid any more trouble. Just before reaching the Sheriff Department, they all agreed to head farther north in the morning to look for new accommodations.

· · · ·

RANDY WATERSON WAS a 24-year veteran of the local sheriff department. He hired on when all that was required was a high school diploma. He was dumber than a box of rocks, but at the time of his hiring, his uncle was the sheriff. Randy was a fuck-up extraordinaire, but his uncle covered for him and did the only logical thing to protect his nephew's career: he promoted him, first to sergeant, and when he was reelected, he promoted him again to lieutenant.

As a sergeant, Randy did as little as possible. As a lieutenant, he somehow did even less. Most shifts, he would drive to the office, read his e-mails, drink a few cups of coffee, flirt with the younger dispatchers, then head home, where he would spend the remainder of his shift unless summoned by his sergeant. On the rare occasion that the sergeant was stupid enough to involve him in something, he would simply say, "You're a damn supervisor, figure it out." He would then go back to watching Netflix.

His uncle was no longer sheriff, but Randy was practically untouchable now as the supervisors were union protected. Unless Randy improperly shot someone, which no way in hell was going to happen because he never did anything, he was invincible.

Randy was alone waiting at the front desk when the Manning brothers walked in. He had been home relaxing when Harley called him several minutes earlier and explained the situation. He reluctantly drove to headquarters. He told the dispatchers if they received a call from anyone complaining about an incident at the Black Bear Tavern to notify him first. He figured the guys might just drive in and smiled at being correct, which was a somewhat rare occurrence for him.

"Good evening, lieutenant," Mitch said, noticing the gold bars on Randy's uniform collar, and held out his hand. "I'm Mitchel Manning and these are my brothers. I'm a police officer in Adrian a bit south of here on the Ohio border." Mitch said while producing his ID and badge in his wallet. "We're up here bowhunting and we were just feloniously assaulted by several patrons, as well as a barmaid, at the Black Bear Tavern. We were also threatened with abduction."

Randy's first thought was, *Fucking Harley didn't tell me one of them involved was a cop.* His second was, *At least the guy isn't a state trooper.* He figured he could handle a city cop or another deputy, but the damn troopers thought they were all gods. Troopers, even if they had no rank, all thought they outranked him!

"I know where Adrian is. I'm sorry to hear about all your problems. We don't usually have much trouble around here. Did any of you get injured?" He asked with mock concern.

Mitch told him that other than minor injuries, they were all fine. He then told him everything that had happened since they arrived, but left out the part about the strange encounter in the woods with the animal, or whatever it was. He didn't want the cop to think they were crazy.

"That is one hell of a story. You boys sound like you're jinxed or something," Randy said after Mitch finished.

"It isn't a story. It's all fact," Preacher interjected.

Randy nodded his head a few times and said, "Well, that is one side of a story. As your brother certainly knows, there are two sides to every story, and I would be in error if I didn't take in both accounts."

Mitch was suddenly not feeling so good about coming to the station. His mood was on the low side even before all that had occurred. His inner instincts were starting to signal alarm bells. He already identified himself as a fellow cop, but the lieutenant wasn't accepting his story as fact. Instead, he seemed to be doubting it.

Ryan spouted off, "Fuck that. A bunch of redneck inbreds almost killed us and you are not doing anything about it. Why haven't you dispatched someone to the bar yet? Don't you want to catch these guys? Are they your buddies or something?"

Mitch grimaced as he knew things were definitely going to get worse now. *Ryan needs to learn to control his mouth,* he thought belatedly and said, "Ryan, that's enough!"

The lieutenant's demeanor went from that of skepticism to one of hostility. His face flushed dark red, and he narrowed his eyes while adjusting his gun belt. Mitch noted his right hand now rested on his pistol's grip. He used his left hand to depress his lapel mic and spoke into it, "Dispatch. Start me a couple of units to the lobby, I'm interviewing several intoxicated suspects regarding a bar disturbance."

Mitch held his hands in front of him and said, "That's not necessary. We're not a threat, nor are we suspects. My brother will apologize."

"Why don't you keep them hands up? In fact, all of you raise your damn hands. I'll decide what you are. As far as checking the tavern, we already received an anonymous call about a disturbance there involving weapons. When my boys arrived, the barmaid was closing up early. She said some tourists started grabbing her tits and ass before some regulars thankfully intervened. She didn't mention any guns but said the little guy in the group went crazy and picked a fight with one of the regulars. It wouldn't be the first time some of our locals got threatened by some visiting hunters that had too much to drink and thought they were better than our residents. Ain't none of you carrying any firearms, I hope." The lieutenant said with an edge to his voice.

Mitch's internal alarm system was wailing so loud in his head now he couldn't think straight. They were in serious trouble if he couldn't smooth this out, and fast. Just then, red and blue lights danced across the lobby's interior as two squad cars skidded to a stop out front. Seconds later, three deputies ran inside assessing the situation. Two of them held tasers while a third had his gun drawn.

The lieutenant grinned widely and said, "Careful. I think some of them may be armed. Search em all and taze the shit out of them if they so much as fucking blink. Oh, one more thing, the little guy wanted you to know they are sophisticated individuals, not inbreds and rednecks like us."

Mitch groaned at the use of the word "little guy" to refer to Ryan and hoped he would let it go, but deep down knew that wouldn't happen.

CHAPTER 40

"Who are you calling little, lard ass?!" Ryan yelled at the lieutenant, ignoring the deputy's pleas behind him to raise his hands. Preacher and Troy had both raised theirs already, along with Mitch.

"Do what he says, Ryan," Mitch said sternly.

Ryan ignored Mitch and said, "Why don't you take off that gun belt and step around that counter and try to take me into custody yourself. I know my rights. I can and will resist an illegal arrest."

The discharge of a taser sounds like that of a small-caliber firearm. Preacher and Troy momentarily thought their brother was shot but Mitch knew the difference and remained calm. Unfortunately, Preacher and Troy did not. They spun around towards the three officers behind them as Ryan screamed and fell forward to the linoleum floor. His body convulsed like that of a seizure victim.

The deputies screamed at Preacher and Troy to remain still, as did Mitch. Preacher now realized that Ryan was tasered, not shot, as he saw the thin copper wires trailing out of the deputy's taser gun to his right. Troy, however, was blinded by rage and charged the officer nearest him.

Once again, a taser was deployed, and the twin metal darts impacted Troy in his upper chest and lower stomach. Mitch and Preacher cringed as Troy now went momentarily rigid from the 50,000 volts before dancing stiffly across the floor and falling to his knees. His resulting scream sounded like the squealing of a pre-teen girl in a haunted house.

The remaining deputy behind them had his actual firearm out and was fanning it between Mitch and Preacher, yelling "Don't move a muscle. I'm not holding a taser. This shoots real bullets."

"For God's sake, relax. I'm a cop too," Mitch said with exasperation.

The officer looked uncertain for a moment but kept his gun level. The lieutenant now walked around the counter and roughly knelt on Ryan's back as he handcuffed him. "Not so tough now, are you, slick?"

"Please, take it easy. He has always had a temper but he's a good kid," Preacher pleaded.

The lieutenant grunted something unintelligible before walking over to Troy and handcuffing him as well. He then approached Mitch and said, "You're a cop, you know the drill. Lean against the counter, hands wide and feet spread." Mitch complied as the lieutenant roughly searched him.

"I'm not carrying. None of us are." Mitch said, thinking how glad he was that once in the parking lot, he secured all the handguns back in the gun safe of his Suburban. He wasn't intoxicated but didn't want to take any chance of jeopardizing his career.

Preacher was searched by one of the other deputies. "He's clean," the deputy said to the lieutenant, then added, "You want them cuffed up as well?"

The lieutenant let out a deep breath before saying, "I suppose not. They cooperated. Lock the other two up for interfering with a police investigation and creating a disturbance."

Mitch sighed as the deputies escorted Ryan and Troy down a long hallway.

"What the fuck, brother? Thanks for the help," Troy said sarcastically as he was escorted past Mitch. Ryan knew he screwed up and remained quiet.

"Look, lieutenant, can we work something out? Is it really necessary to arrest them? I give you my word they won't be any more trouble. We planned on leaving in the morning anyhow. Please. Despite what happened, they are good guys and my brothers. I'm begging you, one cop to another, let me take them home."

"I'm really sorry. You know how it is. Once tasered we have to follow through with our arrest. We are open to liability if we don't. I do not plan on pursuing any charges against you, or your other brother here, as you both wisely cooperated. Perhaps your other brothers should get some anger management counseling. All of this would have been avoided if he didn't come unglued. The barmaid said she didn't want to pursue any charges against any of the suspects, so you can bond your brothers out first thing in the morning. And, since you're a fellow officer, I will release them on a PR bond."

Mitch nodded his head. Preacher asked, "What about the guys that assaulted us? They go free, uncharged?"

Before the lieutenant could answer, Mitch interrupted, "It's okay, lieutenant. We won't be pursuing any charges even if you did find them. It was a huge misunderstanding, and we don't want to trouble you all with it. Do I have your assurance my brothers won't be harmed in here tonight?"

"Of course, of course, this ain't Detroit lockup or any such thing. We're a relatively peaceful community," he replied.

"I appreciate that. I really do," Mitch said while sticking out his hand.

The lieutenant took it and both men shook firmly, eyeing each other carefully. The lieutenant held the grip a bit longer than a usual handshake and said, "One more thing. I don't plan on notifying your chief about this incident unless, of course, you give me a reason to. After all, you probably want to be promoted someday. You have the makings for a decent supervisor, keeping a level head and all during your brothers' arrests."

Mitch stared hard at him while replying, "I appreciate that, but I'm happy being a patrol officer. Riding a desk doesn't suit me."

The lieutenant grinned, then said, "Well, not everyone is cut out to make the big decisions and we need good cops on the beat making the little ones. You take care now." He released the handshake.

Mitch nodded at him and walked out of the building with Preacher following. Once outside, Preacher said, "My God, I think this trip is cursed or something."

Little did he know the worst was yet to come.

CHAPTER 41

The Buford brothers gave Jesse and Karl a ride home in the van. They were all pissed that Harley let the Manning brothers walk. "Your brother is getting soft," the Buford brother who had fought Ryan said.

"Maybe so, but apparently so are you. That little dude kicked your ass!" Jesse answered.

"He got a few lucky punches in. Besides, I was kind of mellowed out from some Vicodin I took earlier."

"Uh-huh," Jesse responded.

Karl and Jesse were seated in the back of the van. "He's right," Karl said to Jesse. "I'm tired of taking orders from Harley. He ain't the fucking boss of me."

"The hell he isn't. You've been his bitch since I've known you guys." The other Buford said.

"Fuck you," Karl said with a sneer.

"Easy, Karl. I'm just voicing my observations from over the years. I'm older than my bro here but we got equal say in any business decisions. Am I lying?" He asked while looking at his brother.

"Nope. You speak the truth," his brother replied.

The driver started to slow down to turn into Karl's driveway, but Karl said, "Keep going."

"Where to?"

"I'm calling an autofill," Karl answered.

"A what?" Jesse inquired.

"An autofill. Fuck Harley. I say we go get them brothers and bring 'em back to the barn."

The Buford brothers and Jesse started laughing. The older Buford said, "I think you meant to say an 'audible.' Not an autofill."

Karl's face reddened in embarrassment. "Fuck all you grammar majors. Whatever. Damn. Let's go get them assholes."

"Look at Karl making his own decisions," the driver teased.

"I don't know if that's a good idea," Jesse said reluctantly.

"Relax, bro. Harley doesn't scare me. We need to take care of these guys. They can identify all of us."

"Where to?" The driver asked again.

Karl admitted he didn't know but figured they were in a rental cabin nearby. He reasoned they could just scout out the larger ones as they probably rented a three-bedroom cabin or larger. That narrowed it down to six possibilities within the immediate area.

They found it on the fifth try. It was the Nitray cabin. Karl knew Mrs. Nitray rented the place out now that her husband died. She lived in Pontiac, Michigan, and rarely traveled north anymore. The Suburban wasn't there but the Bufords' recognized the little guy's pickup. They scouted the cabin, and after discovering it empty, jimmied the rear door. One of the brothers hid the van in a scrub of pines about 100 yards away.

After rummaging around, they found some Bullit Bourbon and some Woody Ales and helped themselves. Jesse produced a pipe and some quality meth from his jacket pocket and fired it up. They all took a couple of hits from it then kicked back in the living room, waiting for the Manning brothers to return.

After 45 minutes of waiting, Karl speculated they went to another bar, but Jesse guessed correctly that they went to the police. Whatever the case, they were going to wait for them, and in the meantime were feeling no pain. They began to make elaborate plans about how they would kill them. The longer they waited, the more drugs they did, and the crazier, and sicker, the plans became.

Finally, at about midnight, headlights illuminated the cabin's interior, and gravel was heard crunching from an approaching vehicle. The four of them were playing poker at the dining room table. They all scrambled like kids playing hide and seek as they ran to separate rooms. Jesse, as planned, ducked out the back door and was going to circle around front after they entered to prevent any retreat.

A minute later, the cabin's front door opened, and Preacher flipped on the kitchen lights. He was followed inside by Mitch, who closed and locked the door. "I'm beat, brother. I'm calling it a night. Do you think we need to worry about them boys from the tavern finding us or can I sleep in peace?" asked Preacher.

"I doubt it. We should be good. Lots of cabin rentals around. In any event, I'll be sleeping, locked and loaded, with one eye open, bro. Just keep your gun in your room loaded, just in case," Mitch answered while opening the fridge to grab a beer.

Just as Mitch was wondering what happened to all the beer that had been in the now-empty fridge, he was processing what his eyes had observed a few seconds ago. The dining room table was littered with empty beer bottles and cards. Mitch was certain that they had cleaned up before heading to the tavern. "Preacher, back door now, run!" Mitch yelled as he swiftly drew his Smith & Wesson .40 caliber from his hip holster just as all three bedroom doors swung open.

"Surprise, you dumb motherfuckers!" Karl yelled as he stepped forward from the bedroom with a one-handed grip on his snub nose .357 pistol. Karl's eyes widened considerably in surprise as he saw only two of the four men they were waiting for, and one of them was already aiming a gun at him from the kitchen.

Time appeared to slow down as it always did for Mitch in an armed encounter. Although he was only involved in one police shooting thus far during his career, there were numerous other encounters when his gun was drawn. Fortunately, those suspects had always wisely surrendered. Mitch realized this was not a surrender situation as his opponents had already made their intentions known earlier at the tavern.

Mitch shot the guy who was holding the .357 twice, center mass, and watched him stumble back into the bedroom. In his peripheral vision, he observed one of the big guys from the tavern lowering a long rifle at him from another bedroom to his right, but Preacher was standing between them and had not yet pulled his pistol from his waistband.

Preacher looked uncertain. Mitch knew he didn't take killing a man lightly, but this was no time to hesitate, Mitch thought. Rather than pull his gun, Preacher charged the big man who was still a few steps away from him, hurling a table lamb at him as he did. The guy reflexively lifted the rifle to block the lamp, and a second later Preacher launched himself at him like a professional swimmer diving in a pool. They tumbled into the bedroom out of Mitch's view.

A handgun barked twice to Mitch's left. He reflexively spun towards the sound just as the flour and sugar canisters on the counter over his left shoulder exploded. Puffs of white powder dispersed in the air. The shots came from the remaining bedroom door where Mitch saw the big guy Ryan had beat up earlier, attempting to lower the huge barrel of a .44 magnum towards him for another shot.

Mitch didn't have time to think how lucky he was that the guy missed both his earlier shots from a distance of only 20 feet away. Instead, he ducked below the kitchen counter as two more rounds sailed above where his head was a second before. The sound of the huge revolver was deafening in the enclosed cabin.

Mitch, now covered in flour and sugar, quickly crab-crawled to the end of the counter, and, leading with his gun, leaned just far enough around the base of it to catch a glimpse of the shooter's left side.

Mitch took careful aim and pulled back the trigger on his pistol. He nailed the big man in his left side before putting a second bullet through his left eye. The guy's head jerked back like it was hit with a ball bat as the back of it splattered the bedroom door. Mitch heard a commotion in the bedroom that Preacher had tackled the other man into. He looked around, then cautiously stood, and started towards the bedroom to help Preacher. He never made it.

CHAPTER 42

J esse ran out the back door of the cabin and circled around the front just as the Suburban rolled to a stop. He crouched down on the side of the cabin in the shadows and watched as two of the guys from the tavern exited the vehicle and trudged toward the front door. *Where were the other two?* He wondered. Maybe they dropped them off at the end of the driveway, suspecting an ambush. The other truck was here so how else would they get home? It wasn't like there were any Ubers around.

Jesse cradled the M-16 that was converted to allow full auto and stayed in the shadows, monitoring the driveway carefully as the two men entered the cabin.

After a couple of minutes, he heard Karl yelling something inside, followed by several gunshots. He risked a peek inside just in time to see one of the Buford brothers get shot in the face. Jesse was mesmerized by how the back of his head was blown out.

The man that shot him was prone on the floor when he took the shot, but now slowly stood up. There was no sign of Karl or the other Buford brother.

Jesse ran to the front door only to discover it was locked. He stood back and kicked it open, splintering the cheap door frame. The man in the kitchen was startled by the noise behind him and swung his way. Jesse was surprised how fast the guy moved. The guy's handgun barrel was almost pointing at him. Jesse let loose with a long volley from the M-16. The man dove behind the kitchen counter but was able to snap off a couple of rounds first.

Jesse saw the flashes of fire spit from the guy's barrel and felt something nip his left ear as the other bullet whistled by the right side of his face like an angry hornet. *Holy shit, the guy almost shot me in the face like he did the Buford brother!* Jesse thought. Jesse was almost certain that he had hit the guy but wasn't about to take anything for granted.

"You bastard! You almost shot me in the face," he screamed while unloading the remainder of the magazine into the kitchen counters. The bullets passed through the rear side of the wood cabinets, shattering bowls and ricocheting off the pots and pans within.

Mitch would have been struck twice in the head by rounds, but by pure coincidence, or providence, he happened to be laying with his head behind the counter that contained a huge cast-iron kettle. A round from the first volley the kid had fired passed through his lower left thigh, fortunately missing his femoral. It burned like hell and blood leaked steadily from the wound onto the tile floor.

Jesse was startled to realize that his magazine was empty just as the guy popped up from behind the counter and pointed his gun at him again. The man pulled the trigger, but nothing happened. He cursed, then frantically tried to clear an apparent malfunction just as the older brother came out of the bedroom pointing a handgun at Jesse. He continued walking towards him and told Jesse to drop the rifle. Jesse did so. Karl came out of another bedroom, pulled back the hammer of his 357, and yelled for the other guy to drop his rifle.

Preacher hesitated, but upon realizing Mitch's gun was hopelessly jammed, he slowly lowered the rifle. Karl smiled at the look of shock upon Mitch's face. Karl ripped open his flannel shirt with his left hand and said, "These bulletproof vests aren't just for cops, asshole, but I ain't forgetting you tried to kill me. Now tell us where the other two are."

"He killed Bubba. Shot him in the face. I saw it from outside," Jesse added. The other Buford brother exited the bedroom that Preacher had tackled him into moments before, blood streaming down his face from a head wound and dripping from his long beard like a leaking faucet. "Who shot Bubba?" he asked.

Jesse pointed at Mitch. The Buford brother glared at Mitch, his eyes filled with hate and fury, but Karl assured him he could get his revenge later. A chime sounded. Jesse fished his cell phone from his pocket, and after looking at the text said, "Oh shit, shit, shit. He's a cop!" He pointed a shaky finger at Mitch.

CHAPTER 43

Mitch's hands were bound tightly with a clothesline. He had been stripped of his clothes except for his black boxer shorts. A heavy engine chain, usually used to lift car engines, was wrapped under the clothesline securing his wrists, suspending him inside the barn. His shoulders ached and burned from the stretched position. Prior to hanging him up, Karl had wrapped some silver duct tape around Mitch's bullet wound; despite this, blood ran slowly from his bare thigh and dripped off his toes that dangled two feet above the oil-stained cement floor. The blood had formed a small maroon puddle beneath him. A tiny stream of it snaked its way to a nearby floor drain.

Mitch was barely conscious but regained most of his bearings after hearing Preacher repeatedly scream in agony. He strained to turn his head to the left to see what was happening to his older brother. Even that simple movement shot stabbing pains down into his shoulders and neck.

He observed that Preacher's wrists and ankles were secured tightly with zip-ties to a metal folding chair. His back was arched and his head thrown back as the chair vibrated in place on the cement floor. Mitch saw jumper cables attached to the legs of the metal chair. The other ends were attached to a huge car-charger that rested on the bench along the far wall. Preacher suddenly quit screaming and slumped sideways in the chair. Drool dripped from his mouth in long stringy gobs as his head hung limply to the side.

The barmaid from the tavern earlier was controlling the charger. She asked excitedly, "Can I zap him again?" while smiling in anticipation. Mitch saw the guy named Karl taking a swig of Wild Turkey straight from the bottle. He wiped his mouth with the back of his other hand and said, "No. Not yet. He's old; we don't want him dying too quickly."

The remaining Buford brother was crushing up something on a nearby table with the bottom handle of his knife. He dipped the tip of the knife into the pulverized powder, then lifted it to his right nostril while pushing his other one closed. He snorted the substance. Immediately, he threw back his head and started yipping like a coyote, then punched his knife hand forward and yelled, "Hot damn! That's really good shit!"

"Take it easy on that crystal. It'll fry what little brain you have left," Karl admonished.

The Buford brother ignored Karl's remark, looked lustily at Sue Ellen, and said, "Come get a taste of this." She started his way, but Jesse grabbed her arm.

"Hey, let her go. She wants to party with a real man," the brother said.

Jesse grabbed his crotch and said, "I got your real man right here, dickhead."

The Buford brother started towards Jesse with his knife outstretched. Jesse snatched up his crossbow from the floor and aimed at the big guy.

"Hey, assholes. Enough already!" Karl yelled,. "We got work to do. It's already 4:30. If Harley gets back and finds this mess, we'll have to kill him too, or he'll kill all of us for sure, especially for killing a cop." The Buford brother lowered his knife. Jesse did the same with the crossbow.

Preacher regained consciousness from the last blast of electricity. "May God have mercy on all of your souls," he said with half-open eyelids. Jesse slapped him hard across the face.

Mitch tried to yell but his words were barely audible. "Leave him alone."

Jesse turned and looked towards Mitch. "Well, look who's finally awake."

The Buford brother now walked menacingly towards Mitch, switching his huge hunting knife from hand to hand as he approached. "You killed my brother."

"Only because he was about to kill me."

"You're going to wish you died that easy, pig!" The brother said.

"Please, let my brother go. He didn't kill anyone. He's a man of God. Kill me if that's what you have to do, but release him."

The Buford brother stopped a couple of feet away from Mitch and smiled. "Not going to happen. You're going to watch your brother die very slowly, and painfully, and then we're going to kill you too, pig."

"You'll have cops all over here. They'll find you and send you all to prison for life. Is that what you want?"

"They gots to have proof and evidence first. Your bodies will never be found. This ain't our first rodeo, asshole," Karl interjected.

"Can we do it now? While they're both awake?" The Buford brother asked Karl.

He nodded his head affirmatively. The Buford brother sheathed his knife and clapped his hands while grinning ear to ear. He yelled, "Shit's about to get real, boys!"

Jesse smiled as he quickly disconnected the jumper cables from the chair and pushed it, with Preacher attached, across the floor. The screeching sound of the metal legs on the concrete echoed about the room. He positioned the chair about 10 feet away from Mitch, then spun it around so both brothers were facing each other.

"Do what? Do what? Sue Ellen asked excitedly while bouncing up and down. Her ample breasts struggled to free themselves beneath her white tank top. Despite the cool air, she was barefoot and wearing cut-off jean shorts so short that the pockets hung below the hem.

"You'll see," Karl said.

"I'll get the bag," the Buford brother said, mesmerized by Sue Ellen's jiggling breasts that were finally settling down. He jogged out of the barn and returned a minute later with a large burlap bag that he held outstretched in front of him. He sat the bag on the floor between the brothers. The top was secured with a zip-tie. Sue Ellen walked towards it but slowed her approach as the bag began to move about on the floor.

"What's inside?" she asked while pointing at it.

"Snakes, seven of 'em. Three of 'em are rattlers, the others big corn snakes," the Buford brother said while giggling nervously.

"Whoa! What are you going to do with them?" Sue Ellen asked with obvious interest.

"We're gonna snake 'im!" Karl said while pointing at Preacher.

CHAPTER 44

Troy and Ryan were placed in separate, but adjoining, holding rooms inside the county jail. They were called "rooms," not "cells," because unlike old school jails, there were no bars. The rear wall of the rooms was cinder block painted a light gray. The front and side walls were thick plexiglass with half-dollar size holes in them.

This was the reason detainees referred to the holding rooms as the "cheese rooms," due to their appearance resembling the Swiss variety. The cramped rooms contained a plastic framed twin bunk bed opposite a stainless-steel commode and hand sink. A small plastic white bench occupied the remaining wall space.

Ryan sat on his bench, leaning over and holding his head in his hands. Troy was stretched out on his bed preparing to sleep. The remaining rooms nearby were empty, but they could hear some unruly guests farther down the hall.

"Try to get some sleep, bro," Troy said.

Without looking up, Ryan responded, "This trip sucks!"

Troy laughed heartily before responding, "You think?! Look, at least we're going to be released in the morning. I know this is only your second time in jail, but I've been in a few and this isn't bad at all. We don't have any roomies. That's a big plus."

Troy had barely finished his sentence when two burly correction officers were heard escorting an unruly inmate their way. A man spewed vicious obscenities at the officers. The officers stopped outside of Ryan's cell. The correction officers were barely able to restrain the wiry man despite both of them being much larger than him. He was pulling and kicking and thrashing about between them, and appeared almost about to break free when one of the correction officers leaned forward and whispered something to him. The thirty-something, wild-eyed man immediately stopped resisting and gazed intently at Ryan, who was still seated on the bench. Ryan gazed into eyes crazier than any pictures of Charles Manson he ever saw.

The man was dressed in the same orange jail jumpsuit as Ryan. He was barefoot and missing most of his front teeth. His head was clean-shaven and had a large scar on the left side, as though his skull had once been cracked. In fact, it had been several years earlier, the result of a drunken ATV accident. The man was a local legend in the county among law enforcement officers. The injury had left him a changed man.

He was a decorated Army Ranger and had planned on being a lifer, but it was on a leave home several years earlier that he had the accident. Afterward, he was a very troubled man who lived with his elderly parents on a quiet lake nearby. At least once a month, he was jailed for a variety of disorderly offenses. On each arrest, numerous officers would be needed to subdue him, as he seemed impervious to pain. Tasers and pepper spray were ineffective. Brute force, and lots of it, was all that controlled him. The officers had nicknamed him Rambo.

"You killed my dog! You killed my damn dog!" Rambo screamed at Ryan as one of the officers punched in a code to open Ryan's door.

"Whoa, whoa. Why are you putting him in with me? The cells across the hall are all empty!" Ryan protested.The guards remained silent as the door slowly slid open. Rambo continued to scream at Ryan about killing his dog. Ryan told him it wasn't him, but the man was working himself into a frenzy. Spittle flew from his mouth and his narrowed eyes bulged as he screamed at Ryan.

"Hey. Hey! You can't put him in there with my brother. The dude's crazy!" Troy yelled at the officers.

They ignored Troy and once Ryan's door was opened, they shoved Rambo forward into the room.

CHAPTER 45

Preacher was fully alert as Jesse grabbed the front collar of his t-shirt and tugged it forward, pulling the thin material several inches away from his throat. Seconds earlier, Jesse had wrapped duct tape around Preacher's waist several times to ensure the shirt remained tight to him.

The Buford brother, using a grabber-type stick similar to those used by the elderly to pick things up, was holding a Massasauga rattlesnake in its plastic tongs, just below its head. The snake rattled its tail nonstop and hissed menacingly as it was maneuvered towards Preacher's neck.

"Easy," Jesse yelled as the head of the snake came close to his hand holding Preacher's shirt collar. When the Buford brother had the snake's tail even with Preacher's face, he began lowering it down into the front of his shirt. When the snake's head was just below the collar, he released the trigger, dropping the snake down the front of Preacher's shirt. Jesse let go of Preacher's shirt collar, which snapped tight to his neck, just as the snake dropped from sight.

"Stay still, brother," Mitch said while locking eyes with Preacher, who looked as though he were holding his breath. The front of Preacher's t-shirt began to move to and fro near his abdomen.

Sue Ellen giggled with excitement, then said, "I think I'm gonna piss myself. Put another one in there."

The Buford brother returned to the burlap bag Karl was holding and lowered the grabber into the bag, retrieving another rattler. This one was even larger than the first one.

"Ooh, baby, that's a big one," Sue Ellen said.

Beads of sweat gathered on Preacher's brow despite the cool interior of the garage. He began whispering the 23rd Psalm while Buford approached him with the second snake. He could feel the cool flesh of the first snake rubbing against his stomach and the head starting to climb upwards against his chest.

The Buford brother held the big snake in front of Mitch, teasingly putting the head near his face. "You scared of snakes, cop?"

Mitch looked into the small reptilian eyes of the rattler as its tiny red tongue darted in and out of its mouth, but remained silent. As the Buford brother dangled the snake slowly in front of him, he said, "This one's for your brother, too. You'll have to wait your turn."

"Actually, it's for you," Mitch replied, and quickly kicked upward, his right foot making contact with the grabber stick. The momentum of the kick knocked the stick upwards and into the Buford brother's face. The attached rattler struck, its huge fangs burying themselves into the man's cheek. It held tight for a moment before both the bar and the snake fell to the floor.

The big man howled in pain and began to dance around, the writhing snake now at his feet. It struck him again in the right calf before Karl ran forward and chopped it in half with an ax he had grabbed from the counter. The two halves of the snake continued to squirm about the floor.

Sue Ellen screamed and pointed at the burlap bag that Karl had let fall to the floor when he retrieved the ax. The remaining five snakes were slithering out, headed in different directions.

Jesse grabbed his crossbow and shot at one just as Sue Ellen took off running for the small pedestrian door, but a snake had wiggled that way.

She quickly veered to the left and hit the button for what she thought was the overhead door, but instead activated the engine chain downward, inadvertently lowering Mitch. She frantically hit another button and the huge garage door began to chug upwards.

Karl charged after another one of the errant snakes with the ax as Jesse tried to load another bolt into his crossbow. Neither noticed that Mitch was now lowered to the floor and was frantically tearing at the clothesline knot attached to his wrists with his teeth.

The Buford brother, holding his face and screaming, followed Sue Ellen out the garage door and into the dark night. Blood dripped from the two puncture wounds in his face and his lower leg was feeling numb.

Mitch freed his hands, grabbed a nearby ball-peen hammer from a workbench, and started towards Jesse, whose back was to him. He wanted to free his brother but knew he had to deal with the others first, or they both would be dead soon. Preacher almost passed out as the rattler's head now peeked out of his shirt collar and started to encircle his neck.

CHAPTER 46

Rambo fell to his hands and knees after being shoved inside the cell. Ryan made the immediate decision to go on the offensive before the enraged lunatic could. He pounced on the man's back and went immediately for a reverse chokehold, his right arm around his throat and his left forearm forcing the back of the man's neck forward. Ryan was astounded that the man easily stood up, then pivoted quickly to his left while dipping forward and flipping Ryan over his head. Ryan landed hard on the stainless-steel commode back first.

It felt as though he had fallen off a two-story building and landed on his back. He heard his spine crack as though a chiropractor had set it, and his lungs emptied of air. His back pain from the earlier fight at the tavern was now tripled. Before he could even think clearly, Rambo was grabbing him roughly and turning him over then forcing his head into the toilet.

Ryan's face was submerged in the bowl's water. Rambo was now leaning onto him with his full weight, yelling, "Die, die, die!"

Ryan panicked as his lungs were already empty from the backflip. He reflexively tried to breathe, taking in nothing but water and began to choke. Troy was screaming for the guards and yelling at the other man to let his brother go while pounding and kicking at the plexiglass wall that separated them.

Ryan flailed his hands about and realized he was about to die. He could not free himself in time from the man's vice-like grip and thought of Frankie and his unborn child. How bizarre a death he was about to experience.

"I killed your fucking dog, not him. I killed your dog!" Troy screamed at the man. Ryan didn't hear this, as he was still submerged in the toilet, but he did feel Rambo release his grasp. Ryan weakly pushed himself off the commode and fell to the floor, coughing and gagging on the water in his lungs. He did this for several seconds, then began to vomit water onto the floor. When he was finally able to breathe normally, he struggled upright and saw the lunatic pounding furiously at the dividing wall between him and Troy. The plexiglass divider was smeared with red streaks from Rambo's bloodied knuckles.

Troy continued to taunt the man. The same two correction officers who put the man in Ryan's room finally approached at a leisurely walk. They were accompanied by two other guards. They assessed the situation, then opened Ryan's cell. They were able to gain control of the deranged man, but it took all four of them to do so and escort him out of Ryan's room. They closed Ryan's cell door, then punched in a code to open Troy's room door.

"No way. No way. Don't put that psycho in here!" Troy cried.

Once the door opened, the guards shoved the man inside. As the door slid to a close, one of them said, "Sleep tight." He winked at Troy and the four shuffled away.

Lt. Waterson was watching everything that transpired on the monitors from the safety of his office. The little punk wouldn't be calling him "lard ass" again. These boys would not mess with him, or his deputies, ever again, that was for sure. His work was done. His corrections officers knew what to do and had so far done it perfectly. They were instructed not to let Rambo kill either of the prisoners, but anything short of that was fine. It was time for him to head home, have a few celebratory beers, call it a night. *That frickin' Harley owes me big time*, he thought.

He had a long history with Harley. When he first became a deputy, he stopped Harley for speeding. Harley happened to be smoking a joint at the time. Harley offered him a hundred-dollar bill to forget the whole thing. The lieutenant acted outraged for a minute, then took the hundred. Hell, a hundred bucks bought a lot of beer back then.

Waterson encountered Harley and Karl regularly after that, as did most of the deputies. The Rowson brothers' reputation was growing steadily among the local law enforcement, and it wasn't a good one. Harley frequently turned to Waterson for assistance in clearing up their troubles with the other deputies. Waterson had to be careful—although Harley paid him well, he wanted to remain a deputy, as he aspired to be sheriff someday.

Yup, Harley owed him big this time. Maybe he would insist on a date with Sue Ellen, he thought. He would love to get into her pants. That would infuriate Karl, but Harley was the boss of that family.

CHAPTER 47

E ach stride Mitch took towards Jesse sent streaks of white-hot pain through his injured thigh. Adrenaline was the only thing keeping him moving despite his considerable amount of blood loss. Jesse, only 12 feet away, was still unaware of his approach and had just loaded another bolt into his crossbow. He finally sensed Mitch's presence and turned his head towards him. The shock on his face was matched only by Mitch's rage.

Jesse frantically tried to spin around to shoot Mitch with the crossbow, but Mitch had already started to swing the hammer in a wide arch. The hammer connected with Jesse's left temple with a satisfying crunch. The head of it was buried a full three inches into the side of Jesse's brain.

Jesse's eyes snapped wide open but were unseeing. Mitch wrenched the hammer from the side of his head. Dark maroon blood mixed with clear fluid leaked from the crater where his temple had been. Jesse collapsed face-first onto the dirty concrete floor. His face cracked, but he didn't feel anything, as he was already dead.

Preacher saw Mitch dispatch Jesse and now observed that Karl saw the same thing. Karl began to run towards Mitch with his ax reared back. The snake was curled around Preacher's neck with its head resting on his shoulder. Preacher wanted to yell a warning to Mitch but feared the sudden noise would cause the snake to strike him. Instead, Preacher prayed harder for deliverance for his brother from the evil all around them.

Mitch sensed movement in his peripheral vision at the last possible second. As he turned, he saw the outstretched ax coming downwards towards his head. Mitch realized he couldn't backpedal fast enough, so he stepped towards Karl instead.

He knew the ax was on a perfect trajectory towards his head, so by stepping into the downward blow, he gambled it would go over his head and strike his back instead. Not ideal, but better than the alternative.

The ax indeed went over his head, and partially pierced his upper back below his left deltoid. The blow was painful but certainly not lethal. Mitch rocked his head backward and forcefully snapped it forward into Karl's face, shattering his already busted nose and knocking him off balance. Karl staggered into Preacher's chair and fell onto his lap.

The rattler responded to the sudden intrusion with a heavy bite into the side of Karl's neck. He screamed and dropped his ax before falling forward to the concrete floor. The snake uncoiled itself from Preacher's neck and slithered down him to the floor, where it zigzagged across it before disappearing underneath the workbench.

Mitch walked over to Karl with the ball-peen hammer still in his hand.

"Help me! Please help me. You said you're a man of God!" Karl pleaded while holding his left hand over his neck wounds, still kneeling on the floor.

"I said he's a man of God," Mitch said while pointing at Preacher. "Me, I've lapsed a bit with my faith. I hope to get it back soon, but not today."

Mitch reared back his hammer to strike Karl in the head, but stopped short when Preacher shouted, "No! That's enough, brother. He's done."

Mitch, still holding the hammer raised over his head, glanced at Preacher with indecision edged all over his face.

"I said that's enough, brother. Now please get these restraints off me."

Mitch's depression was close to its peak. He didn't care about himself, let alone the worthless scum before him, but his brother's respect for him still mattered. He sighed and tossed the hammer across the room. He grabbed a folding knife from a sheath on Karl's belt, then walked over to Preacher, cutting loose his restraints.

Karl pushed himself up to a seated position and said, "I don't feel so well. My neck is cold, but my face feels on fire." He started to puke onto the floor.

"Tell someone that gives a shit!" Mitch replied coldly.

Mitch helped Preacher to his feet. "We gotta get out of here, brother. That crazy woman or big guy could be back any second," Preacher said.

"I think the big guy is done for. He was bit twice, but that woman could still be an issue," Mitch said while limping over to a nearby workbench to retrieve his pants. He grimaced as he pulled them on, Preacher keeping a lookout near the open door. He slipped on his boots.

Preacher approached him with a roll of duct tape from the workbench. "Let me do a quick patch on your back. That ax opened it up a bit." Preacher liberally poured the remaining vodka that was used earlier to sterilize Jesse's finger over the cut, then wrapped the tape around Mitch's torso a few times. He then helped Mitch put on his shirt.

"Thanks, bro. We better roll." Mitch grabbed a tire-iron from the workbench and scooped up Jesse's crossbow from the floor. Both men were exhausted and pale.

"You okay, brother? Can you make it?" Preacher inquired.

"Never better. Hell, I was only shot once, and that ax only nicked me." Mitch smiled while handing Preacher the cross-bow. "How about you?"

"I could have done without being half-electrocuted but thank God that rattler didn't bite me."

Mitch nodded his head. "That was freaky. I didn't know you were a snake charmer."

"Believe me, it had nothing to do with me. I don't know why, but I think we'll be okay now."

"I love your optimism, brother, even if I don't share it at the moment."

They started to walk out of the barn towards the driveway when headlights started bouncing towards them. Mitch could barely discern the shape of the wrecker that had towed him and Ryan just yesterday approaching. The crazy woman exited the rear of the home, holding a handgun in one hand and restraining a massive dog in the other.

Karl crawled from the barn and yelled, "They killed Jesse!" He then collapsed, dead.

Sue Ellen now spotted the Manning brothers on the far side of the barn. "You motherfuckers!" She screamed while pointing at them and yelling to Buttlicker, "Tear 'em up!" before releasing him. She now took a two-handed grip on the big gun and began firing wildly at them.

"This your idea of things getting better, bro?!" Mitch said with urgency as they turned around and began running for the rear of the property, the huge dog lumbering after them and bullets whistling overhead.

CHAPTER 48

Troy stood in the far corner of his cell in a classic fighter's stance, body quartered away from his opponent, leading with his left fist held high and the right low. Rambo had worked himself into such a frenzy that he was practically hyperventilating. Troy was scared shitless. He had been in several fights in his life, and won a few of them, but only if his opponent was drunker than he was. The crazy energy radiating off his new cellmate was like static electricity. Troy could actually feel it.

The roles were reversed with the brothers, as now Ryan yelled suggestions at Troy. "Kick him in the nuts!" screamed Ryan. "Don't go toe to toe with this guy. He's freakishly strong!"

Rambo screamed and charged Troy with his hands spread far apart. Troy attempted a straight kick to his groin, but it glanced off the side of his thigh instead. Rambo slammed Troy back-first into the concrete block that comprised the rear wall. With his left hand, he held Troy's forehead against the wall as tight as if it were in a vice. He slipped his right forearm underneath Troy's chin and began to push it forward into Troy's Adam's apple. Troy started to kick his feet wildly and rained punches onto the side of the man's face and body as he felt the pressure steadily increasing against his neck. Troy's efforts appeared to have no effect on the madman.

"You killed my dog! You killed my damn dog!" The lunatic wailed as he continued to lean all his weight onto his forearm pressing against Troy's neck.

Troy was now in pure panic mode as he struggled for air. He felt that his throat was about to collapse. He couldn't quite make out what Ryan was yelling. Something about "the guys" over and over. Troy's vision began to tunnel, and his hearing started to lower as the lack of oxygen reduced his senses. He looked deeply into the madman's eyes with resignation to the inevitable, when he suddenly realized what Ryan was screaming over and over: "eyes," not "guys!"

With every last ounce of energy, Troy lifted both his hands to his attacker's face and spread his fingers wide on each side of his head while slowly pressing his thumbs, firmly and forcefully, into each of the man's eye sockets.

Mitch had shown Ryan and Troy this technique several years earlier after attending a self-defense seminar by a former Russian Spetsnaz officer. It was very painful and effective when nothing else worked. Hopefully, the attacker released his grasp before his eyes ruptured. If not, reasoned the former Spetsnaz officer with a shrug, he would never see the error of his ways, or anything ever again.

Rambo was definitely in the latter group as he continued pressure on Troy's windpipe despite thumbs being pressed into his eyes. Troy ramped up the pressure of his thumbs until Rambo's eyes ruptured. Troy felt a pop like a balloon squeezed too hard. Vitreous fluid and blood leaked from his sockets as the crazy man finally released his chokehold on Troy and staggered backward, howling in pain. Troy collapsed against the bed frame, massaging his neck while breathing in large ragged gulps of precious air.

The four guards hustled down the hall and piled into the cell. Two of them roughly handcuffed Troy while the other two guided Rambo to the bench. The four guards looked panic-stricken.

"This is all on you. It's on all of you!" Ryan screamed. "My brother's a cop. All of you should be in one of these cells, not us!"

"What the holy hell is going on here?!" A deep voice boomed off the walls.

The Manning brothers saw that the voice belonged to an extremely fit middle-aged man that looked as though he could be cast as a Navy SEAL in an action thriller. He was wearing workout clothes and carried a gym bag.

The four guards collectively gulped and one of them finally stuttered, "Eve-eve-evening sheriff. This guy," the guard stuttered while pointing towards Troy, "just popped Rambo's eyes out."

"Judas Priest. I can see that, but why in the hell were they in the same holding room? Everyone knows what Rambo is capable of and for that reason is always isolated."

"Um, we probably should speak with our union rep before we answer that." One of them interjected as the other three quickly bobbed their heads in agreement.

"That is probably the first intelligent thing any of you have said today!" The sheriff yelled, then clenched his jaw and gave all of them a withering glare.

CHAPTER 49

Harley and Snake jumped from the wrecker. Sue Ellen was firing wildly at two shadowy figures running behind the barn while Karl, illuminated in their headlights 25 feet away, appeared to be dead in the driveway. Deeper inside the barn, Harley saw Jesse lying on the cement floor with a huge pool of dark blood gathered about his disfigured head.

Snake ran to check on Karl and Jesse while Harley ran up to Sue Ellen, who was still repeatedly pulling on the trigger of her now empty handgun. Harley gently forced the gun downward while asking, "Sue Ellen, what the fuck is going on?"

"They killed your brothers, and the Buford brothers too."

"Who killed them?"

"The guys from the tavern. Well, two of the guys, not all of them."

What the hell is going on? Harley thought. Lt. Waterson had texted him earlier and assured him the matter was handled. Two of the brothers were in jail and the other two were released primarily because one of them was a cop.

Harley looked towards Snake, who was walking back towards him. Snake somberly shook his head and made a cutting motion across his throat with his hand. "I'm sorry, but they're both dead. Someone smashed the side of Jesse's head in, and Karl looks like he was bit by a rattlesnake."

"They're getting away. Go after them!" Sue Ellen yelled hysterically.

"Do they have any guns?" Harley asked.

"I don't think so."

Buttlicker was barking in the distance but suddenly yelped in obvious pain. A few seconds later, he limped past them towards the house, favoring his right front leg.

Snake jogged to his van that was still parked in the driveway and returned with an M-15 and a 12-gage. Harley grabbed the shotgun from him and ran into the barn, returning with two heavy-duty flashlights.

"Call Randy and tell him to get out here ASAP. Don't call dispatch, call his cell directly. Tell him what happened and that we need his help now. The number's on the fridge," Harley said to Sue Ellen, who was now crying hysterically. Harley grabbed her and roughly slapped her. "Do it now!" Sue Ellen nodded her head several times and started walking towards the house.

"What a cluster fuck. What the hell happened here?" Harley asked Snake, not expecting an answer.

"It looks like your brothers were torturing a couple of them. There are some zip ties next to a chair and under the hoist is a pool of blood and some cut rope. I think the guys escaped somehow," Snake said with a shrug of his shoulders.

"Come on. We got to get them before they can contact anyone, especially the cop. The last thing we need is a bunch of state cops here. These motherfuckers killed both my brothers!" Harley said, then started jogging towards the back fence 50 yards away.

• • • •

MITCH AND PREACHER ran about 50 yards before encountering a six feet tall privacy fence topped with barbedwire. "Dammit," Mitch hissed. "You first, and hurry, that dog's coming." He bent over and cupped his hands to give Preacher a foothold up the fence.

Preacher placed the crossbow down on the ground and stepped into Mitch's hands. He grabbed the top strand of barbed wire and pulled himself up until his waist was even with the top wire. He gingerly extended his right leg over the top of the barbs and pivoted the remainder of his body over the top, but his trailing pant leg snagged on a barb. He yanked at it while upside-down, and it suddenly came loose, causing him to slam into the opposite side of the fence face-first before bouncing off of it and landing hard on his back on the ground.

"You okay, bro?"

"Perfect, I'm just perfect." Preacher said with obvious sarcasm.

Mitch pitched the crossbow over the fence, as well as the tire iron, before starting up the fence. He was only halfway up when a huge shadow lunged from the darkness and sunk its teeth into the ankle of his left boot. The dog was growling and shaking its head back and forth while completely suspended off the ground. Mitch was shocked at how heavy the dog was as his grasp on the fence broke free and he tumbled back to the ground.

The dog immediately released its grip on his ankle and scrambled up his torso. Mitch felt its long nails dig into his stomach and saw its jagged, yellowed, sharp incisors as its mouth opened wide. Its breath was rancid. Its snout dipped towards his neck as the dog went for his throat. Mitch, still on his back, dipped his chin forward to protect his neck, while swinging hard with a short right hook into the side of the big dog's head just as it was about to bite his face. The punch pushed the snout away from his face momentarily. Mitch grabbed the dog's left front paw and snapped it upwards violently. The dog yelped in pain before retreating into the shadows.

"Would you quit playing with that dog and get over the fence, brother?" Preacher said in an exasperated tone.

Mitch rolled onto his stomach and slowly pushed himself upright. "Playing with the dog! Seriously."

Preacher grinned back at him, then looked concerned again and said in an urgent half-whisper, "Hurry, brother, they're coming."

Mitch turned around and saw two flashlight beams bouncing towards them. He threw himself onto the fence again, and, despite his exhaustion and wounds, was fueled by a fresh adrenaline dump. He was up and over it within a few seconds.

"That's how you clear a fence, brother," Mitch said with a grin. "Now give me that crossbow. I don't want you to have to kill someone."

Ignoring him, Preacher knelt down and raised the crossbow, carefully aiming through the fence. "I'm a Catholic Deacon, not an Amish Elder. I got this. Now get moving. I'll be right behind you."

Mitch patted him once on the shoulder and said, "Don't die on me," then started limping through the thick brush towards what he hoped would eventually be the river. Some illumination from a full moon aided his departure into the swamp.

CHAPTER 50

Lt. Waterson was in his personal vehicle, a 2019 Chevy Silverado. He had barely understood Sue Ellen on the phone a few minutes earlier as she was crying hysterically. He eventually calmed her down enough to learn that Karl and Jesse, as well as both Buford brothers, had all been murdered—allegedly by the Adrian cop, and his brother, that was in his police station several hours earlier.

To make matters even worse, as soon as he got off the phone with her, one of the correction officers on duty phoned him and told him what had happened at the jail with Rambo. The sheriff was also aware and was on a warpath. What a total clusterfuck beyond imagination!

Waterson reached into his center console, grabbed a bottle of Tylenol, and dry swallowed three of them. He had one hell of a headache coming on. After fish-tailing his pickup into Harley's driveway, he roared through the open gate towards the home.

Sue Ellen stood on the porch in black spandex pants and a two-sizes-too-small orange spandex sports top. Despite the circumstances, Waterson was tempted to take advantage of the situation. He had tried on several occasions to get in her pants but was always rebuffed. He climbed down from his truck and walked towards her, unconsciously smoothing his thinning hair over his ever-increasing bald spot while sucking in his gut.

"Thank God you're here. Harley and Massey went after them and have been gone for about 15 minutes now. I heard a couple of gunshots about 10 minutes ago but nothing since then. Those guys are dangerous. They killed everyone!" Sue Ellen said and started to sob hysterically.

Randy quickly wrapped her up in a hug, pulling her against him. She didn't resist. He felt her big breasts smash against his chest. He deeply inhaled her scent. She smelled like lilacs, or at least her hair did. He lowered his right hand and cupped her lower butt with it. It was firm, no flab.

He felt himself begin to get aroused, as apparently did she. Sue Ellen pushed quickly away from him and screamed, "You filthy pig. My boyfriend lies dead in the driveway 30 feet away and you grab my ass?! You're disgusting!"

"Now, now, Sue Ellen. I sincerely apologize but I'm a man after all, and when I felt your body pressed against mine, I..." He said with upturned palms.

"That's no excuse. Us gals are not taking your guys' shit anymore. I could get your ass fired for that."

"Seriously, Sue Ellen. I'm here to help you out with what sounds like an accessory to murder, as well as abduction, and you are threatening to report me for grabbing your ass? I'll tell you what. When I finish up here and help you all out, you are going to owe me big time, and I'm going to collect. Understood?" Waterson said with his face turning red.

Sue Ellen made a face like she ate spoiled fish, then crossed her arms and said, "Whatever, but so far you ain't done shit for me."

"First of all, I'm going to drag Karl's body into the barn. Afterward, I'm going to lock it up. After that, I'm driving out of here and you're going to lock the gate up behind me, then go in the house and lock it up too. Those boys might try to double back. I doubt it, but just in case, have a gun ready."

"Where are you gonna go?"

"I'm going to head down the road and wait for Harley and Snake to flush them out. The most logical way out is to follow the river. I sure doubt they'll try to cross it. I'll be waiting for them if Harley and Massey don't get them first. If I see them, I'm going to put them down like a couple of wounded deer. We can work up some type of story bout how they came here to rape you, and the boys tried to intervene. The tourists killed them, but Harley and Massey gave chase and flushed them out to me. They opened fire on me, and I had to shoot 'em."

Sue Ellen bobbed her head then said, "That might work."

Randy continued, "Hell, you all will be heroes, and me too. I suppose it'll make me a shoo-in for sheriff at the next election, catching quadruple murderers and all. Play your cards right and I'll make you my secretary. You can work dayshift for a change and have health care, and even have a pension."

"Huh. Dayshift and a pension. I don't know much about computers and that stuff."

"You can learn. Hell, I bet you got all kinds of other skills. I mean, you'll make 30 grand a year."

"Thirty grand! That sounds good."

"Good enough to forget that 'Me Too' nonsense?" Waterson asked with a grin.

"Maybe," Sue Ellen said with a slow smile.

CHAPTER 51

Two of the four correction officers decided to talk after conferring with their union rep by phone. Their accounts of the incident corroborated what Ryan and Troy had already told the sheriff. The sheriff was shocked to learn that Mitch Manning was their brother. He attended the same police academy as Mitch many years prior.

They finished first and second in their class. He respected Mitch back then, and after a quick early morning call to his current chief, respected him even more. His chief had nothing but high praise for him.

Once he realized Lt. Waterson was involved in the mix, the sheriff began to understand how things had gotten so out of hand. He resented Waterson from the day he started, and the feeling was certainly mutual. In his opinion, Lt. Waterson was the antithesis of what a law enforcement officer should represent. If not for a strong union, he would have terminated Waterson on the day he was elected sheriff.

His department was now looking at a possible multi-count lawsuit because of yet another inexcusable decision by Randy. The sheriff decided to release the Manning brothers on their own recognizance. He told them a more thorough investigation would be completed, but for now, both men were free to go.

When he realized they were unable to contact their brothers to arrange for pickup, he offered to personally drive them to their rental cabin. The three of them piled into his new Jeep Gladiator and headed east towards the cabin. The dark black

220

sky was starting to turn a pale purple as the sun was close to rising. There was no other traffic on the lonely roadway at this hour. The only sound was the aggressive tread of the Michelin tires emanating from their contact with the asphalt.

"We appreciate what you're doing for us, Sheriff," Ryan said.

"Please, call me Brock. I apologize again for the actions of Lt. Waterson and the correction officers. From the preliminary investigation, it's fairly obvious to me that some bad decisions were made by some of my men. I fully intend to make certain that those mistakes are never repeated again."

"I can see why you guys call that guy Rambo. He almost killed both of us," Troy interjected.

"He wasn't always like that. It's a damn shame the way he turned out. The guy was a local legend, in a good way, for many years, but after his accident, he was a different animal altogether. In fact, every so often he puts on this freaking wolf costume and runs around Dogman Swamp scaring the bejesus out of people. I'm shocked he hasn't been shot yet. I reckon he won't be doing that anymore," Brock said while looking at Troy in the rearview mirror.

"Wait! Does he still do that?" Ryan asked.

"Oh, hell yes. All the time. He would often wait until dark then run across the road in front of a car just far enough not to get hit but certain to be seen. He would also sneak up on kids that were parked back in the swamp lookout and then jump on the hood of their car. He probably prevented a lot of unwanted teen pregnancies, 'cause them boys were probably impotent after that for a long time," Brock said with a chuckle.

"How did you know it was him?" Troy asked, leaning forward to hear better.

"He got his foot caught in an illegal bear trap a couple of years back. He screamed so loud, and in such agony, that a local trapper heard him from over three-quarters of a mile away. When he came upon him, Rambo had his mask off and was trying to get the trap off his nearly severed foot. The trapper snapped a couple of cell phone pics while his buddy helped Rambo out of the trap.

"I'm surprised you hadn't heard about that. It made CNN for one night. Thing is, once his foot was repaired, he was back at it. He's learned to mimic the scream he did when he caught his foot in the bear trap. You should hear him. It's the worst scream I've ever heard."

Troy and Ryan started laughing.

"Hey. I'm serious. It's terrifying just hearing him scream."

"We believe you. We both encountered him a couple of days ago. We thought it was the Dogman," Ryan said, still laughing.

"Well, there ya go. So, you heard the scream too?"

"Hell yes, we did," Ryan said, leaving the part out that he shot at him several times.

"We think the same assholes, I mean, the same fine local residents, that harassed you at the tavern paid him to do it. We've suspected them for numerous illegal activities on their property that is bordered by the swamp. It makes sense for them to try to frighten folks away, so no one stumbles upon their illicit activities." The sheriff said as he drove past Lt. Waterson's personal vehicle. "That's weird," he mumbled.

"What is?" asked Troy.

"That truck we just passed parked on the berm belongs to Lt. Waterson."

"Is he a hunter?" asked Ryan.

"Not that I know of."

"Our cabin is just a mile ahead. The drive is on the right side of the road." Troy offered.

As they pulled up to the cabin, all of them saw the busted front door standing wide open and the windows on the west side shattered. Stranger yet was that hundreds of crows were perched on the cabin's roof, gutters, and nearby trees.

"Oh, shit!" Troy remarked, recalling his dream on the plane.

"I'm guessing that wasn't like that when you were last here?" Brock asked.

"No, sir, but that's both our vehicles," Ryan answered.

"Wait here until I check it out."

Brock exited and grabbed a 12-gage Remington 870 from behind the rear seat. He racked in a round and started forward, calling out for Mitch and his brother while identifying himself as the sheriff. He tactically advanced to the cabin, utilizing trees and the parked vehicles as cover. The crows became agitated as he neared, "caw cawing" and taking little nervous steps and hops about the roof.

Once at the door he did a quick peek inside. He saw the interior of the cabin was in disarray. Chairs were toppled and the kitchen cupboards were riddled with bullet holes. Blood spatters and smears were everywhere. He cautiously entered and conducted a slow, methodical check of the interior. When he ensured that all was clear, he returned to the truck where the brothers were anxiously awaiting. The crows became increasingly agitated.

"Is everything okay?" both asked at once.

"No one is inside, but there are signs of a shooting, and there is blood everywhere," he said evenly with an intense look.

The Manning brothers were too shocked to speak.

Brock grabbed his portable radio from his glove box and called into his dispatch for additional units to the location. The purple haze of the Eastern sky was now mixed with an orange-reddish glow and, for some reason, made Brock think of the fires of Hell.

CHAPTER 52

Snake reached the fence first, as Harley had stumbled just before getting there. He shone his flashlight along the edge of it and started walking the perimeter. He only walked about thirty yards when he saw some blood droplets on the grass. Looking up, he spotted a small piece of material snagged in one of the barbs. *Just like tracking a wounded deer*, he thought.

"They crossed the fence here," Snake said pointing at the blood and fabric, as Harley caught up to him. Harley nodded his head and handed Snake his rifle to hold while he scaled the fence. Harley was half over the barbed-wire when he heard a twang. A second later, Snake grunted. Harley looked down at him. Snake just stood there, motionless, staring straight ahead. Harley continued over the fence and dropped softly to his feet on the other side. The horizon continued to lighten, as did the darkness around them.

"You okay?" He whispered as Snake stood perfectly still, looking straight ahead, as though frozen in place. Harley was about to say something else when he saw what appeared to be a hole in the center of Snake's neck. Wordlessly, he fell backward, landing on the pine needle covered ground like a felled oak tree.

• • • •

PREACHER SAW THE HUGE Native American man from the tavern locate the exact spot they had climbed over the fence. A few seconds later, he was joined by the guy that had allowed them to leave the tavern, who was now scaling the fence.

Preacher had no doubt what the two planned to do to him and Mitch if they found them. Despite this, he still found it difficult to do what he was about to do.

He sighted the compound on the huge man's upper chest. He figured it was better to take him out with the one arrow left, rather than the smaller guy, especially since the Native American was now holding both rifles. "Forgive me, Lord," Preacher said to himself as he pulled the trigger. The bolt shot forward, towards, and through, the chain-link fence. At first, he thought he missed him completely, until, after a few interminable seconds, the huge man toppled backward to the ground with a solid *thunk*.

Preacher realized the other guy had now dropped to his side of the fence but did not have his rifle as both rifles were now on the opposite side. He knew Mitch wouldn't be able to move very fast for very long, due to his injuries. Preacher decided now was the time to end this. He set the now useless bow aside and bolted from the underbrush, charging the man at the fence with the tire iron Mitch had left with him.

Harley, still in shock at Snake's death, was a bit slow responding to the rustling he heard behind him. He spun around just in time to see the older of the men from the tavern charging towards him with a tire iron. The guy was swinging the tire iron in a wide arc parallel to the ground, aiming for his ribs. Harley flung himself back into the fence as the metal bar barely missed him. The fence boomeranged him forward into his attacker.

Both of them tumbled to the ground and rolled over while clutching each other. Harley roughly headbutted the man, then kneed him in the groin. These blows allowed him to break free from the man's grasp. Harley jumped up and stepped backward before withdrawing his Randall machete from his sheath attached to his belt. All woodsmen worth their salt were familiar with Randall hunting knives. The exorbitantly priced hand-crafted knives were among the best in the world. The machetes were no different and had an edge on them like a Samurai sword.

Preacher lost his tire iron. He groggily stood up, warily eyeing the man standing just 15 feet away from him. Time seemed to slow considerably for Preacher as he assessed the situation. He scanned the ground for the tire iron but instead saw a short section of a dead tree limb between him and the other man. It was his only chance.

Preacher knew he couldn't outrun him. "Heavenly Father, give me the strength to defeat this man," he said to himself as he lunged for the limb. He bent low, grasped one end of it with his right hand, and swung it up violently, connecting with Harley's groin just as Harley swung the machete downward. It severed Preacher's arm just below the elbow.

Preacher remained standing as Harley fell to the ground before him. He was shocked at the lack of pain, as he gazed at his forearm and hand on the ground. Blood started to gush from his remaining upper arm, showering Harley, who was still on his knees.

Preacher staggered backward. He began squeezing his bicep with his other hand to try to stem the flow of blood as he turned and stumbled headlong into the swamp. While running, Preacher removed his belt and quickly slipped it over his injured arm just above the damage, yanking it tight while looping it around his upper arm several times. He managed to tuck the loose end of the belt into a crease as he continued forward.

Pine branches slapped across his face as he frantically made his way towards the river. The bleeding slowed to a steady drizzle but easily marked his trail for Harley, who was now pursuing him. The pain came on like a tidal wave and completely overtook him. He stumbled but remained upright, remembering his drill sergeant from decades earlier hollering, "Pain is weakness leaving the body." If that was indeed true, Preacher thought, he never realized how much weakness was within him.

CHAPTER 53

Sheriff Brock instructed the Manning brothers to stay at the cabin property but not to go inside or disturb anything. He was playing a hunch and going to check on Lt. Waterson. He assured the brothers that his crime scene techs would arrive within the hour and the remainder of his deputies would be checking the homestead of the suspects.

Immediately after the sheriff left, the hundreds of crows that were assembled flew off all at once. They resembled a huge black storm cloud that floated quickly away just above the trees.

"What the heck was up with all those crows? I've never seen that many flock together," Ryan remarked.

"It's a murder, not a flock."

"Say what?"

Troy repeated, "A group of crows is called a murder, not a flock."

"Huh. That's creepy as hell."

Troy recalled his nightmare once again and involuntarily shivered. He said, "Screw this. I'm not sitting around waiting while Preacher and Mitch are in trouble."

"Me neither, bro. What do you suggest?"

"I think they've escaped from those freaks and will be coming to the river from the opposite side, and need help crossing it," he replied with a tone of certainty.

"What makes you think that?" Ryan said with skepticism.

Troy sighed and said, "I'll explain later, brother, but just trust me, and whatever you do, don't go into the river."

Ryan looked at Troy quizzically.

"I mean it. Don't go into that water, no matter what! We need to stay on this side of the river, that way we won't interfere with the sheriff and his guys."

"Whatever, bro. I don't intend to go into that river. That water is probably only 50 degrees and it's flowing quick. Let's do it. Should we gun up?"

"Hell yes, but I better stick to a shotgun. I don't have a CCW like you do."

"Sounds good," Ryan said while walking to Mitch's truck. He pulled on the rear hatch, and both doors were locked. "I figured he locked it."

Troy walked to the side of the cabin and grabbed a large piece of decorative concrete edging from the flowerbed. Ryan shook his head and said, "Mitch ain't gonna be happy about this."

Troy smiled as he pitched the chunk of concrete through the passenger side window, then reached inside and popped the locks. "He'll get over it."

Ryan opened the safe, luckily remembering the combo from the previous evening. He grabbed his handgun and the extra magazine. Troy grabbed Mitch's 12-gage and shoved extra shells for it in his jacket pocket.

Dawn had arrived. It was now practically full light. The brothers went around to the rear of the cabin and started walking towards the river, looking carefully for blood or other signs of their brothers.

"Be careful. If a deputy happens to be on this side of the river, he may very well mistake us for those assholes," Troy warned.

"Copy that, bro. I'm going to go a bit left so we can cover more ground. Holler if you see anything."

"Will do. At least we don't have to worry about the Dogman anymore," Troy answered.

Ryan just shook his head, still embarrassed he had fallen for it. *Wait until I tell Mitch about it,* he thought. He would never hear the end of it.

• • • •

MITCH WAS RUNNING OUT of gas quickly. He was emotionally and physically drained, His adrenaline dump had worn off. His entire body was one big mass of pain. Blood was seeping from his wounds and he had already lost a lot of it at the barn.

He slumped against a tree and slowly slid down to a sitting position. He was done. Tears started to roll down his cheeks as he realized he was going to die in the swamp. He wiped them away with his hands, embarrassed he was crying even though he was dying. He said a short prayer asking God for forgiveness for not being a better Christian and asked that he look over his brothers and protect them. He prayed for his daughter and regretted not having spent even more time with her. He closed his eyes. He could feel his body shutting down. It was a visceral feeling from previously unknown depths.

"Get up, son. Your daughter needs her father and your brothers will need you in the future."

Mitch could not believe his ears. It was his father's voice, but his father had died several years ago. He slowly opened his eyes. No one was there. He looked all around. Nobody!

Moments earlier, he was too weak to be of any assistance to anybody, but now, buoyed by his father's words—whether an auditory hallucination or something else all-together un-explainable—he pushed himself upright and willed himself to trudge forward. After just a few minutes, he reached the river's edge and waited, hoping that Preacher would stumble out soon. Was he even still alive? Did they capture him?

Mitch turned around to look back into the swamp and then heard a loud rifle shot to his left. The impact of the bullet through his left abdomen spun him around. He stumbled and slipped down the riverbank into the icy cold water of the Au Sable. Its strong current carried him, face-first, downstream like a capsized canoe.

CHAPTER 54

Lt. Waterson was nestled against a large white pine that had been blown over a couple of years ago along the riverbank near the top of a slight rise. He rested his 30-30 lever-action Winchester on top of the tree and scanned the riverbank below his location with the attached Leupold VX-5HD scope.

Randy wasn't much of a deer hunter, but virtually every male, and a large percentage of females, that resided in the northern half of lower Michigan owned a hunting rifle. A northern Michigan home without at least one hunting rifle would be akin to a Russian home without a bottle of vodka in the cupboard.

Randy chose the perfect spot. It was only a couple hundred yards from the main road and at the edge of the swamp where it finally thinned enough for someone to traverse it. He was confident the brothers would eventually wind up at the riverbank and follow it back towards the road if Massey and Harley didn't get to them first.

He didn't have to wait too long, as just a few minutes after settling, a figure emerged from the edge of the swamp less than 150 yards away. He squinted into the scope. Fortunately, it was now light enough to see decently through it. It was the cop! The guy looked half-dead already. Waterson took careful aim at the middle of his chest, center mass, and gently squeezed back the trigger.

The shot echoed off the surrounding trees as the rifle slammed back into his shoulder. He was happy to see the guy spin around and fall into the river. *Bingo! One down,* he thought to himself. He settled back into position to await the other brother. He could already see tomorrow's headline in their county paper: "Hero Deputy Hunts Down Multiple Murder Suspects."

• • • •

SHERIFF BROCK PARKED behind Lt. Waterson's truck and grabbed his shotgun before stealthily entering the edge of the swamp near the riverbank. He was about 50 yards in when he heard a rifle shot not too far off in front of him. "Dammit," he swore to himself as he hurried along that way.

• • • •

RYAN HEARD THE RIFLE shot. It sounded close but was probably from the other side of the river. He scrambled forward but stopped short of stepping into a small clearing adjacent to the river. He knelt down near a small bush and scanned the riverbank but didn't see anything at first. Then he saw a log drifting down the middle of the river coming towards him. As it neared, he realized it was a body.

The body floated directly in front of him and was just fifty feet away. He realized with abject horror it was Mitch. Without hesitation, he darted forward, running headlong into the frigid waters. He was up to his waist, and just about to dive forward, when he heard someone shout something, followed by a second shot. His left shoulder felt as though he was struck with a sledgehammer. The rifle slug went straight through, exiting his upper back.

• • • •

SHERIFF BROCK SAW MOVEMENT 20 yards ahead, amid a deadfall. He stopped and realized it was Waterson with his back to him. He was sighting through a rifle at a man running into the river from the opposite bank about 150 yards away. "Don't do it!" Brock yelled, but the rifle's report pierced the otherwise quiet swamp and the man fell down into the water with a splash. Waterson spun around and was quickly racking in another round as Brock raised his shotgun and took aim. "Drop it, Randy!"

Randy hesitated, then quickly jerked the rifle up to take aim at Brock. Brock fired twice before Waterson could pull his trigger. Eight of the double-aught buck pellets struck Waterson in the chest and face. His body was thrown back against the tree before crumpling to the ground. The sheriff advanced carefully with a third shell now chambered. When he was within 20 feet it was apparent Waterson was dead, as one pellet left a near-perfect pencil sized entry wound between his eyes, and two others had entered his forehead.

Brock whispered regretfully, "Good Lord, Randy, what did you make me do?" as he slowly shook his head. Remembering the man shot in the river, Brock began running downstream along the riverbank. Unfortunately, the guy was now over 200 yards away and floating downstream quickly. Randy grabbed his portable radio and informed dispatch that shots were fired, and two men were struck and at least one was deceased. He requested air support from the Michigan State Police as well. He gave his GPS coordinates to facilitate an emergency response, then continued jogging along the riverbank.

CHAPTER 55

Harley struggled to his feet. The kick to his groin nearly caused him to lose consciousness. Upon standing, he felt a sudden wave of nausea and doubled over to empty the contents of his stomach. He wiped the vomit from his lips, then smiled at seeing Preacher's severed arm. He would be even easier to track now. He grabbed the bloodstained machete off the ground and started forward, determined to make the two brothers pay for killing his only family.

• • • •

TROY HEARD THE RIFLE shots, and what sounded like a shotgun discharge, seconds later. He ran forward towards the river, stumbling over mossy stumps and leaf-covered roots. His heart was threatening to explode from his chest as he continued. He caught glimpses of the wide, quickly flowing river ahead. The darkness of the water resembled flowing black marble.

He reached the riverbank and saw Preacher kneeling on the opposite side, his head bowed and his arms at his side. *No, no, please God no!* Troy thought as he realized Preacher was missing half of his right arm.

"Preacher!" he screamed with tears flowing down his face. Preacher slowly lifted his head and their eyes met across the wide river. Preacher looked hopeless, like an ugly mutt in the pound with no chance of rescue. The early stages of shock were setting it.

"Preacher. I'm coming to you. Don't move," Troy screamed while half sobbing.

Troy caught movement in the river in his peripheral vision. He turned that way and saw two bodies in the middle of the river floating towards him. The first was Mitch, face-down in the water and unmoving. The other one, about 10 yards behind, was Ryan, He was flailing about with only one arm struggling to stay afloat and to get to shore.

Troy looked desperately between the three of his brothers, each one needing his immediate aid. His mind, unable to prioritize who needed help first, froze him in place. It couldn't possibly get any worse—until it did.

A blood-covered man holding a machete emerged from the thick swamp only thirty feet behind Preacher. Troy barely recognized him as the man from the tavern who had ordered the others to release them the prior evening. It was readily apparent he had opposite intentions now.

Troy raised his shotgun and aimed, but Preacher was in the way, and it was too far a shot for the shotgun. The pellet pattern would be too wide and likely strike his brother as well. Preacher must have heard the man approaching, as Troy saw him turn around before turning back to Troy. He looked at peace now, no longer scared but resigned to his fate. He said exactly what Troy knew he was going to say.

"Save your brothers. I'm already dead!"

Troy finally snapped out of his momentary paralysis and ran forward to the river, tossing aside his shotgun just before diving into the breathtakingly cold water. He swam towards Mitch and caught up to him quickly. He flipped him over onto his back and stroked strongly back towards the riverbank.

Troy started yelling into Mitch's ear. "Don't you die on me, brother, dammit, don't you die. Please, God, don't let him die." He heard another shotgun blast, very close, but was too focused on the task at hand to worry about it.

He reached the riverbank and hauled Mitch onto the grass. He glanced back towards where Preacher was. Sheriff Brock was kneeling next to him with his arm around his shoulders. The blood-covered man was sprawled on the ground behind them.

Troy heard his brother Ryan yelling for help, as he drifted past him, now losing his battle with trying to stay afloat. "Hang on brother. Hang on!" Troy screamed while quickly doing some deep chest compressions on Mitch, then administering two quick rescue breaths. Once completed, he rolled Mitch on his side before sprinting back to the riverbank and diving in again.

He reached Ryan quickly and realized Ryan had been shot just below the shoulder. That arm was useless. "I got you, brother. I got you. Hang in there, buddy." Troy now said another silent prayer to help him get his other brother to safety, as well as one for Mitch to live. He side-stroked towards the shore, fighting the strong current. Ryan, too weak to speak, simply nodded his head and clung tightly to Troy. When they finally reached the safety of the riverbank, he dragged Ryan to the grass and gently laid him down.

Troy now observed several uniformed deputies approaching and saw another doing CPR on Mitch. He glanced at the other side of the river. Preacher now had a solar blanket wrapped around his shoulders. He weakly waved to him with his only hand. Troy waved back.

"It's going to be okay. You're safe now," an approaching female deputy reassured him.

He heard someone coughing and gasping for air. When he realized it was Mitch, he began to sob once again and simply said, "Thank you." The deputy mistakenly thought Troy was talking to her.

Troy looked upwards into a clear blue sky. The last remnants of darkness had diminished, and the early morning sun sent tendrils of light through the towering pines. A solitary bald eagle, its wings spread wide, completed a lazy circle above them. Not a single crow was in sight.

EPILOGUE (SIX MONTHS LATER)

"What an absolutely horrific experience all of you went through," the most popular daytime talk show host in America said while shaking her head and dabbing her eyes with a tissue.

Mitch and his brothers reluctantly agreed to the interview after being besieged by virtually every major network for the past several months. Troy finally persuaded them. The price was right, and he was low on gambling funds again. The DiCarlo brothers were threatening him again despite him paying off the majority of his outstanding debt.

"You guys are heroes. Each and every one of you!" she continued as her studio audience burst into applause. After they quieted down, she smiled warmly at them and said to Preacher, "I understand that you have 80 percent of the use of your arm back now. That's amazing."

Preacher nodded his head and said, "Yes." He raised his hand and made a fist. "I certainly don't have too strong a handshake anymore but besides that, it's fine."

"Thank God the deputies found it, and the surgeons were skilled enough to reattach it."

"Thank God, indeed." Preacher echoed her statement while gazing upward.

"And Mitch, you endured 13 surgeries and five months of rehab, but you're considering returning to your police job in a couple of months?"

"I am. I'm feeling stronger every day. Besides, I only have two more years before I can collect my pension. I still enjoy it despite most of the mass media painting us in a poor light. Not all of us are bad, but yes, there are a few bad apples, as in any profession."

"Well said. And, Ryan, you were shot just below the shoulder with a high-powered rifle. How are you doing?"

Ryan raised his arm but stopped at shoulder level. "I can only get it this high, but other than that, I'm good," he said with a goofy grin.

"And finally, last but not least, Troy. You saved two of your brother's lives. How does that make you feel?"

"Besides them teasing me constantly as the only one not getting seriously injured, I would say I'm doing well," he replied as both the audience and host laughed.

"Brothers will be brothers, no matter what their age," the host replied.

"Seriously, though, this trip, although tragic, brought all of us closer together than we have been in years. I haven't always been a good brother and have done things I have seriously regretted. Our dad kept us close, even during my screwups, by insisting on our annual camp together." Troy had to pause now as he was starting to choke up.

Mitch, seated next to him, placed his arm around him and whispered, "I love you, brother. It's all forgiven, We're good. We're brothers."

Troy nodded his head and said to the host, "I don't know what I would do without my brothers."

The host, with tears streaming down her face, stood and applauded the brothers as the audience joined her in a standing ovation. "I have a surprise for you guys. Actually, a couple surprises. I'm going to bring another guest to tell you about the first one. Would everybody please welcome to our show Sheriff Brock Kendall from Lake County Michigan!"

Brock walked out, waving to the applauding audience. He embraced the host, then shook all of the Manning brothers' hands. The host directed him to a seat near her.

"Sheriff Kendall, it is an honor to meet you," she said when the audience finally quieted down.

"Please, call me Brock, ma'am," he said warmly.

"I understand you have some news you would like to share with the Manning Brothers."

"I do," the sheriff said while turning in his seat to face the brothers. "Ryan and Troy, I'm happy to inform you that we will be dropping all charges previously filed against you both."

Ryan and Troy smiled widely before Ryan said, "Thanks, sheriff. Thank you so very much." Troy nodded his head vigorously in agreement.

"After a thorough investigation, our department understood you were unduly provoked by a command officer of ours and that Troy acted in self-defense of his life when attacked by another inmate. A few of our correction officers exercised extremely poor judgement in carrying out an unlawful order given by the same command officer. Two of those correction officers are no longer employed with our agency and the remaining two were disciplined. Please once again accept my sincerest apology for all of their actions."

"We understand, Sheriff, and thank you for all you have done for us," Mitch said.

"Sheriff—I'm sorry, I mean Brock. The command officer you were referring to, is he the one that you had to shoot?" The host asked.

"Yes, ma'am. Unfortunately, I did have to do that as he had just shot Ryan and was turning his weapon on me."

"And then just a few moments later, you had to shoot another man that was about to do additional harm to Luke Manning, or Preacher, as his brothers call him."

"Yes. The man was coming at Preacher with a machete in a threatening manner and had already harmed him with it once."

The host was shaking her head slowly while biting her lower lip. "Thank God you were there, Brock. I can't begin to fathom what all of you endured that terrible day. Please, everyone, give these brave men another round of applause."

The audience erupted into cheers, whistles, and claps for almost two full minutes. When they finally quieted down, the host said, "Before we close out our show, I have another surprise for you guys. I understand that despite the horrific experience of your last hunting trip, you are all still planning on going deer hunting together again this year, correct?"

"We certainly are," Mitch answered. "Despite last year, it is always the highlight of our year. We couldn't imagine giving it up."

"Excellent. I know this will upset some of my viewers, but frankly, like I told our producers, I don't care. My father and brothers were hunters and I ate my fair share of rabbit and pheasant growing up that they harvested. I personally see nothing wrong with ethical hunting but respect those who disagree with me. I have arranged a week-long hunting trip, all expenses paid, for all of you during the last week of October in the Upper Peninsula of Michigan on 500 private acres, with a deluxe cabin near the Porcupine Mountains."

The audience started to applaud but the host motioned for them to stay quiet. "And best of all, hunting celebrity Gus Powers will be joining you. He'll be filming your hunts, and exploits, for an upcoming episode of his wildly popular series, *Big Bad Bucks*!" The host beamed.

The Manning brothers exchanged smiles, and Ryan, speaking for them all, enthusiastically said, "Hell yeah! Does the sheriff get to join us?"

"He certainly does, if he wants to."

Brock nodded his head and said, "It would be my pleasure and an honor to hunt with all of you."

• • • •

SUE ELLEN WAS MESMERIZED by the program. She leaned forward in her chair, listening to every word. She was lucky to have followed her instinct and fled the home as soon as Lt. Waterson left. She used the ATV to escape, taking advantage of the numerous backwoods trails until she reached a truck stop. Getting transportation from truckers all the way to California was no problem. It was a long-haul ride none of them would ever forget or mention to their wives.

Once in LA, she found work as a stripper and was soon discovered by a Mexican Cartel leader who happened to be making a rare appearance in the U.S. He was immediately smitten with her.

"Carlos, sweetheart," she said urgently to her soon-to-be husband, who was sitting next to her reading a magazine. "It's them. Those are the bastards that killed my friends."

Carlos set the magazine on his lap and watched the program with her. Afterward, he remarked, "It sounds like your friends were not very nice people."

"I'm sorry, baby, but didn't I see you just last week cut a man in half with a fucking chain saw?!" Sue Ellen said angrily.

"But that was business. I often have to make an example of those that are disloyal to me. It seems like your friends tried to kill these men for foolish reasons. That is different."

"I'm telling you my friends were good men. Now, these assholes are smearing their names even more. You keep telling me you'll give me anything I want if I marry you. Well. I want them dead. All of them!"

"I don't know. This is not a good idea. They did not harm you, my sweet."

"They gang-raped me in the bathroom of the tavern," she lied. "I didn't want to tell you that. I didn't want you to feel differently about me," Sue Ellen said while doing her best to look sad and truthful.

The cartel leader clenched his fists and narrowed his eyes as a solitary vein pulsed in the middle of his forehead. "Luiz!" He yelled.

A tall, fit, Hispanic man promptly entered the living room. "Yes, Carlos?"

"I need you to plan a trip to the Porcupine Mountains in Michigan's Upper Peninsula for the last week of October. Take as many men as you need to eliminate four brothers. I will get you additional information soon."

"Yes, sir," he said and exited the room.

"I'm so sorry this happened to you. These men will pay with their lives for hurting you," Carlos said while stroking her hair and kissing her forehead.

"Thank you," Sue Ellen said while taking his hand and leading him towards their bedroom.

• • • •

IT HAD BEEN A WEEK since his TV appearance. Sheriff Brock stood in front of his truck near the edge of Dogman Swamp where he had abruptly stopped after seeing something dart across the road. It was big and hairy, not as large as a bear, but close. It appeared to have been running upright. He looked over the pines at the full moon shining brightly when an ear-piercing scream pierced the otherwise quiet night. The small hairs at the base of his neck felt electrified.

He knew Rambo was in lock-up again; despite his blindness, he was still getting into trouble. Another scream responded to the first one from the opposite side of the road. Brock, feeling extremely uneasy now, got back in his truck. *Some things defy a rational explanation and are better off left alone,* he thought, as he shifted into drive and drove quickly away from the swamp.

The End

Acknowledgments:

Special thanks to my copy editor, Danielle Mohrbach. I certainly tested her skills.

Thank you as well to Mark Mohrbach, Randy Harris, Norm Perreault, Kathy Stone, and Jeff Wagner for reading the original manuscript and offering their suggestions to improve it.

Thank you to my wife Cindy for the numerous hours that she allowed me to spend in my writer's den typing away.

Lastly, thank you to my brothers, Richard, Mark, and Ken, as well as my cousin, Jeff Wagner, for giving me inspiration and encouragement to write this novel. Like the fictional Manning brothers, we make an annual trek to northern Michigan in pursuit of whitetail deer. Fortunately for us, our trips are far less harrowing.

Don't miss out!

Visit the website below and you can sign up to receive emails whenever Tom Mohrbach publishes a new book. There's no charge and no obligation.

https://books2read.com/r/B-A-QWLH-BVMJB

BOOKS 2 READ

Connecting independent readers to independent writers.

Also by Tom Mohrbach

Vatican Vengeance
Cardinal Deceit

Standalone
Vatican Vengeance
Northern Nightmare

Watch for more at https://tommohrbach.com.

About the Author

Tom is a retired police sergeant with 30 years of law enforcement experience from Monroe, Michigan. He was also a weekly columnist for the Monroe Evening News featuring his personal police stories.

Northern Nightmare is his third novel. He currently resides in New Port Richey, Florida, with his wife, Cindy.

You can follow Tom on his Facebook page Tom Mohrbach Novels or go to his website at, tommohrbach.com

Read more at https://tommohrbach.com.

Made in the USA
Monee, IL
16 November 2021